"Hal and Jean-Pierre have found Hildegarde."

"Good. She's alive?"

"Alive but not happy, I think."

"Are they bringing her in?"

"That's the problem, Commander. She appears to be naked or almost naked and tied to a wooden frame on a cart drawn by a couple of longhorns. She is near the head of a column of heavily armed and mounted warriors coming this way. Hal and Jean-Pierre haven't gone in close. They have laser rifles in the hovercar, of course. They have grounded the car in a hollow about three kilometers ahead of the column. They don't think they were seen. Hal spotted the column when it was about six or seven kilometers away."

"What is the strength of these bastards?"

"About a thousand. They are sending in the Immortals. . . ."

Fawcett Gold Medal Books
by Richard Avery:

THE EXPENDABLES

#1   THE DEATHWORMS OF KRATOS

#2   THE RINGS OF TANTALUS

#3   THE WAR GAMES OF ZELOS

THE EXPENDABLES #3

The War Games Of Zelos
Richard Avery

A FAWCETT GOLD MEDAL BOOK

Fawcett Publications, Inc., Greenwich, Connecticut

THE EXPENDABLES #3

THE WAR GAMES OF ZELOS

Copyright © 1975 by Richard Avery

Printed in the United States of America

First printing: December 1975

1   2   3   4   5   6   7   8   9   10

Stage One

DISCOVERY

Stage Two

CONTACT

Stage Three

THE WAR GAMES

This one is for Shaun,
whose passion for War Games
took me to Zelos.

R.A.

Stage One

DISCOVERY

MEMORANDUM

To: Secretary General, United Nations.
From: Director, Extra-Solar Planets Evaluating and
         Normalizing Department.
Subject: Résumé of ExPEND operations.
Date: 6th November 2077 S.E.T.

Para 1. The construction of the F.T.L. vessel *Golden Hind*
has now been completed. Proving jumps to the vicinities
of Alpha Centauri, Sirius, and Procyon will take place
throughout the first eight months of 2078 S.E.T. Upon
successful completion of the programme, command of the
vessel will be given to Captain Yuri Litvinov, late of the
United Nations Space Service. His team will include the
veteran Expendables Fidel Batista (ref. File One, Appen-
dix Two, ExPEND Report, December '73), Chantana Le
Gros (same ref.), and Ruth Zonis (ref. File Two, Ap-
pendix Two, ExPEND Report, March '76). Captain
Litvinov's mission will be to prove the second planet of
Alpha Tauri (Aldebaran), designated as Janus.

Para 2. Meanwhile, after refit and approved modification,
the *Santa Maria* has now proceeded to investigate the
colonization potential of the fifth planet of Alpha Piscis
Australis (Fomalhaut), distance 24 light-years. This
planet is now designated as Zelos.

Para 3. Telemetry carried out by robot probe indicated

that Zelos has an E-type biosphere based on normal oxygen and carbon cycles. The planet is smaller than Terra, but the marginally reduced G-field should present no problem. No signs of radio emission, technological development, or abnormal radioactivity have been registered. It is therefore reasonable to assume the absence of an advanced culture. If Zelos can be proved suitable for colonization, computer estimates indicate that it could ultimately support one thousand million human beings.

Para 4. The team of Expendables assigned to the Zelos project is led by Commander James Conrad who, as you know, has already distinguished himself in the proving of the planets Kratos and Tantalus. I append to this memorandum further details concerning Commander Conrad and the present complement of the *Santa Maria.* I am most optimistic about the outcome of this present project. A man who can successfully meet the challenge of the death worms of Kratos and the rings of Tantalus should experience little difficulty in proving Zelos—a planet which does not appear to have any special complications.

Para 5. The colony already established on Kratos continues to expand. Latest information indicates that the population of Jamestown is in the region of 6,000, with approximately 750 being indigenously born. Iron and copper are being mined, and an oil well is on stream. A small refinery is already operating. Another town is under construction.

Para 6. On Tantalus, the population of Kheladelphia is approaching 2,700. However, this figure includes approximately 250 scientists of various disciplines and nationalities who were transmitted to Tantalus by your authorization to investigate the remains of the ring system. Upon completion of their studies they will, of course, be returned to Terra. Preliminary reports indicate that the defunct colony of aliens had a highly sophisticated culture and were technologically and scientifically well ahead of our own culture. It is not yet known from which part of the galaxy they came, but the surviving fragments of their star maps suggest that their planet of origin must be several hundred light-years away. I understand that the investigations of the ring system have already revealed several revolutionary technological developments which may find application in the solar system.

Para 7. It is anticipated that, within ten years, both Kratos and Tantalus will be exporting to Terra, via matter-transmission, substantial quantities of elements now rare or very difficult to obtain in this system. Surveys indicate that there is an abundance of gold and platinum on Kratos, and that Tantalus has a rich diamond-bearing region. Mining operations for the aforementioned do not yet have local priority, the immediate task being that of making the colonists self-sustaining. But it is already clear that in the foreseeable future there will be a considerable return on investment in the ExPEND projects. This fact alone will be of use in neutralizing/silencing the remaining critics of the programme.

APPENDIX I

Complement of *Santa Maria* re proving of Planet Five, Alpha Piscis Australis (Fomalhaut), aforementioned planet, now designated as Zelos.

Conrad, James. Age 42. Commander Expendables, Team Three. Nationality: British. Ex-commander United Nations Space Service, formerly captain. Distinguished Space Service Cross and Bar. Resigned from U.N.S.S. after being reduced to rank of commander and forfeiting ten years' seniority as a result of court-martial. Court-martial findings (presided over by Admiral Kotuzov): guilty as charged of wilfully and repeatedly disobeying orders of commanding officer when permission to attempt rescue of crew of S.S. *Einstein* in decaying solar orbit was denied; not guilty of putting at risk safety of S.S. *Gagarin* which he then commanded; guilty of bringing about the deaths of three of his crew members and one engineer officer in aforementioned attempted rescue. Conrad himself was badly injured in the incident. One arm was severed by a mooring cable, and one eye was burned out by solar radiation. Now has prosthetic right arm and infrared eye implanted in vacant right socket. The artificial eye is normally covered by a silver patch. Awarded Grand Cross of Gagarin for services rendered on Kratos.

Smith, Indira. Age 34. Second in command, Expendables, Team Three. Nationality: Indian. Ex-surgeon, Lieutenant, Terran Disaster Corps. Resigned commission following torture and severe injuries inflicted by terrorists in Brazil. Now has prosthetic legs. Awarded Distinguished Space Service Cross for Services rendered on Kratos.

Kwango, Kurt. Age 37. Ecologist, Expendables, Team Three. Nationality: Nigerian. Previously convicted criminal with history of violence. Behaviour since recruitment by ExPEND irreproachable. Granted free pardon for crimes committed. Awarded U.N. Gold Medallion for services rendered on Kratos, and the Polaris Star for services rendered on Tantalus.

Mencken, Hal Joseph. Age 32. Engineer, felon. Nationality: American. Convicted by Canadian court for murder in Montreal. Volunteer Expendable. Released from prison under U.N. Mandate 31-B-9-72 and placed in custody of ExPEND for indefinite period.

Dolfuss, Hildegarde. Age 29. Biochemist, felon. Nationality: Austrian. Convicted by British court of inflicting grievous bodily harm on another person, and of dangerous driving, resulting in the death of two people. Volunteer Expendable. Released from prison under U.N. Mandate 31-B-9-72 and placed in custody of ExPEND for indefinite period.

Gautier, Jean-Pierre. Age 30. Weapons and explosives expert, felon. Nationality: French. Convicted by Monagesque court of theft at Monte Carlo. Volunteer Expendable. Released from prison under U.N. Mandate 31-B-9-72 and placed in custody of ExPEND for indefinite period.

Ustinov, Jane. Age 27. Marinologist, felon. Nationality: South African. Convicted by U.S. court of kidnapping and blackmail in New York. Released from prison under U.N. Mandate 31-B-9-72 and placed in custody of ExPEND for indefinite period.

APPENDIX II

Though the science of robotics has advanced considerably since Commander Conrad set out to prove the planet

Kratos, he decided—against the advice of the experts—to take six models of the S.P.9 series for the Zelos project.

In particular, he insisted on the presence of S.P.9/1, designated as Matthew. This robot is now technically obsolete, a more flexible model having been developed. However, Commander Conrad chose to ignore the advice of the experts, his argument roughly being that the devil you know is better than the one you don't know.

As you are aware, the S.P.10 series has already been tested exhaustively in adverse conditions on Terra, Luna, and Mars. These robots are undoubtedly superior in performance and flexibility to the previous series. One significant difference is that the S.P.10/1 is capable of making independent value judgements and acting upon such judgements. For example, if the commander of a proving expedition and a team member were in a dangerous situation where only one of them could be saved, a self programming Ten robot would save the commander, regardless of the order, or orders, it received.

This function Commander Conrad views with great distrust, maintaining that only a human being has the right to make such decisions. Psychiatric investigation has revealed that Commander Conrad has mildly paranoid tendencies. The report indicates that his hostility to S.P.10 robots is directly related to fear of having his authority usurped or challenged.

Because of his record re Kratos and Tantalus, I deem it necessary to humour him on this occasion. But, as you know, substantial funds and resources have been devoted to the development and perfection of the S.P.10 series. I therefore propose to assign six S.P.10 models to Captain Litvinov for the proving of Janus. When the *Santa Maria* and the *Golden Hind* return upon completion of their missions, an evaluation of robotic performance will be carried out. Despite his record, Commander Conrad cannot be allowed to obstruct progress.

Phase One

OUT OF THE COOLER

Conrad opened his eyes and groaned. He didn't like what he saw. He couldn't make any sense out of it. The colours and the shapes were all one horrible mess. His mind recoiled from the effort of trying to interpret the visual data. He groaned once more and tried to move his arms. They would not respond.

Something was placed over one eye. He knew what it was. A silver patch. He remembered that much. Now he was able to focus, to interpret what he could see.

There was a robot bending over him. It had the word "Matthew" painted on its chest plate. Now Conrad knew what was happening. He was coming out of the big cold. It had happened before. He ought to be used to the trauma, but he wasn't.

Matthew massaged his chest with thermal gloves. Conrad was immensely grateful for the radiant heat.

"Sir," said Matthew, "are you in a condition to receive data?"

Conrad thought about that. It took some time and effort. Still, memory was returning. There was always a temporary amnesia after suspended animation, but it seemed as if he was developing some kind of tolerance. When Matthew had resuscitated him in the Kratos orbit, it had been pretty rough for a time. Tantalus had been better; and this time orientation was taking place quite rapidly. He had already remembered about the patch, his own name, and fragments of his history. He knew that he was a spaceman, that he was in the resuscitation chamber of a starship called the *Santa Maria* and that Matthew, the metal monster, was an old friend.

It was a pity that human beings—in the conscious condition—could not survive faster-than-light drive without going crazy. It was fortunate that robots could. They weren't programmed to go crazy. They were programmed to reject nightmares, visions, phantasms, and all the gremlins that seemed to proliferate in subspace. Robots didn't feel or imagine or create. They only thought. Electronically. Maybe they were lucky. Maybe not.

The word "Zelos" floated into Conrad's mind. He didn't know what it meant, but it was a trigger mechanism. "Yes, I am in a condition to receive data."

"Decision noted. Sir, you are James Conrad, commander of the faster-than-light vessel *Santa Maria*. The vessel is now in stable orbit round the planet Alpha Piscis Australis Five, designated as Zelos by the Extra-Solar Planets Evaluating and Normalizing Department of the United Nations. Your mission is to prove Zelos for human colonization. Your personnel consists of six human beings and six self-programming robots. I am S.P.9/1, designated as Matthew for your convenience. Do you read me?"

"I read you." It was all coming back fast now, remarkably fast. Experimentally, Conrad tried to move his arms once more. He managed to move one of them—the prosthetic arm. He should have known that would be the one to respond first. "How long will it be before I am operational?"

"Your reactions are very good, Commander. Revised estimate is forty minutes S.E.T., plus or minus five percent." Indefatigably, Matthew continued with the thermal massage.

"Make it faster. I hate this place."

"Query, sir: Is the situation designated as an emergency?"

"No, damn you!" snapped Conrad irritably.

"Then, Commander, I must proceed normally. I am not empowered to put your life at risk."

Conrad stared at the walls of the resuscitation chamber and at the battery of radiant heat lamps that beamed energy to the key areas of his body. He felt much-needed heat rising up also from the fluidized bed on the intensive care bench where he lay. Soon his still half-frozen body would be able to move without too much pain. But what would take the chill out of his soul? Nothing the clever boys back on Terra could devise. Maybe there was a limit to the number of times you could freeze people without making them flip. No doubt the problem had been researched. ExPEND was, at least, thorough. And, anyway the trauma of resuscitation was better than the traumn of F.T.L. drive.

Conrad's intense hatred of resuscitation procedure somehow gave strength to his mind and body. He hated lying naked, defenceless, while some bloody machine executed a programme that would make him human again. The hatred produced anger, and anger boosted the flow of adrenalin.

With his prosthetic arm, he pushed the robot's gloved hands away. Then, somehow, suppressing a groan as messages of pain from all the stiff muscles overloaded his central nervous system, he managed to sit up.

"I want a large brandy. Have one sent up quick!"

"Sir, I am not empowered at this stage—"

"Shut up and execute!"

"Query: Is the situation now designated as an emergency?"

"Yes, blast your miserable circuits, it is!"

"Decision noted," said Matthew gravely. "Execution proceeds. Mark has been assigned. The brandy, designated as Hennessey XO, amount four fluid ounces, will be available in approximately two point two five minutes. Is that satisfactory?"

"It's tolerable," conceded Conrad grudgingly.

"Sir," said Matthew with a faint, metallic note of protest. "This is a most unusual procedure and not to be generally recommended for the resuscitation programme."

"Life," retorted Conrad, "is a most unusual procedure. But what the hell would you know about that? Now get on with the thermal massage and beat that forty-minute estimate. That is an order."

"Decision noted. Execution proceeds."

Later, as Conrad was sipping the brandy and enjoying the luxurious feeling of warmth flowing back into his limbs, Matthew said surprisingly, "Commander, in this situation, I am empowered to point out that you are a real mean bastard."

Conrad looked at·him, amazed. Then he did some rapid thinking. Finally, he said, "Who had that interesting mandate inserted into your programme?"

"Mr. Kwango, Commander. It was inserted during my second proving trial on Terra. His rationale was that during a period of stress, the statement would have a beneficial effect upon you. Resuscitation procedure is defined as a period of stress. Does the statement have a beneficial effect?"

Suddenly, Conrad began to laugh. Kwango, the black joker, had struck again. He felt at home.

"Yes, Matthew, the statement has a beneficial effect. How long before I can put on my clothes, eat a decent meal, and get sensible?"

"Approximately seventeen minutes, Commander. Your responses are very good."

Conrad finished his brandy and leaned back. He didn't feel cold anymore. "Then keep up the good work, Matthew. When you have finished with me, take Lieutenant Smith and Mr. Kwango out of the cooler. Leave the others for a while. I want to spend a little time alone with old friends."

"Decision noted, Commander. Execution proceeds."

Phase Two

SO THERE AIN'T NO PEOPLE!

Conrad felt relaxed and content. He was in the saloon with Lieutenant Smith and Kurt Kwango. They were just finishing an enormous and luxurious meal consisting of genuine Scotch steak, real dirt-grown vegetables, a good red wine, cheese and biscuits, fruit, coffee, and brandy.

Coming out of suspended animation always left a person immediately and ravenously hungry. Conrad was secretly pleased that he had managed to contain his hunger until Indira and Kwango were operational. The meal had been worth waiting for, and it had given him much more pleasure than the mere consumption of food ever could.

Among the three of them, a very special relationship had developed. This friendship had been forged in danger, crisis, adversity. It had survived the death worms of Kratos and the rings of Tantalus. It was durable.

"Boss," said Kwango, helping himself to another large brandy, "you've gone dead silent. Most unusual. It disturbs me. Normally, you are spitting out so many words, we all get dazed trying to ignore you . . . What are you thinking about?"

"I was thinking," lied Conrad, "of fining you one booze ration for tampering with Matthew's programme. At the worst it could be construed as sabotage, at the best as insubordination."

Kwango shook with silent laughter.

Indira said, "You are a bloody awful liar, James."

Conrad sighed. "I know. It is not one of my strong points."

"Anyway, what has Kurt done to Matthew's programme?"

"He taught that goddam robot to call me, quote, 'a real mean bastard,' unquote. Under the articles of Space Service, that is—"

"But it's the truth," cut in Indira, managing to remain solemn. "You *are* a real mean bastard, James Conrad. Is Kurt to be penalized for programming our command robot with accurate data?"

"Lieutenant Smith," said Conrad, attempting to sound severe, "it is not for you to criticize the judgement of your commanding officer."

Indira also took more brandy. "Come off it, James. Shall I give Kurt a blow-by-blow account of what happened at Applecross? Now, what were you *really* thinking?"

Conrad also reached for the brandy bulb and squirted expertly into his mouth. "Well, if you must know—and I will deny all knowledge of this conversation later—I was thinking about the three of us and how we somehow fit together. We survived on Kratos, we survived on Tantalus —will we survive on Zelos?"

Kwango gazed at him in amazement. Then he burst out laughing. "Boss, *you* are the only kamikaze pilot on this mission. The good Lieutenant and myself are the back-up system. When you hit the deck at a great rate of knots, we just pick up the pieces and put them back together. That's how it was on Kratos. That's how it was on Tantalus. We are getting used to it, so not to worry. Besides, this planet ain't got no death worms, it ain't got no nasty rings and it ain't got no people. Have some more booze, and stop worrying. It interferes with my digestive processes."

Indira said, "An attack of the vapours, James? I simply don't believe it. Mood indigo, perhaps?"

Conrad smiled. "Mood indigo, I suppose. You and this stupid black bastard are my kind of people. Maybe it makes me feel a special responsibility—which, logically, is absurd. I know Zelos should not present any unanticipated problems. The probes say so. Virgin planet, untouched by bug-eyed monsters or human hands . . . Maybe I'm just getting old, but it all seems too neat."

"Ho, ho," scoffed Kwango. "Senile is the word, Boss. Now you want to play de great white father. . . . Lieutenant, this man is unfit for duty by virtue of paranoia. Relieve him of his command, I'll countersign, and then we'll stick him back in the cooler and prove Zelos ourselves. How's that?"

"Dreadful," retorted Conrad, before Indira could speak. "Kurt, I'll bet you have the worst sense of humour within a radius of fifty light-years."

"Since it is obvious that your mind is crumbling, Commander, sir," said Kwango, "I will ignore that remark."

Indira said, "Stop behaving like children, the pair of you. . . . I know what you are trying to say, James. But we have always known that the tough Commander Conrad has a heart. Take it easy. We're all expendable. That's why we're here."

"Lieutenant," snapped Conrad, rapidly changing mood,

"we didn't survive on Kratos or Tantalus by taking it easy. Zelos looks O.K., but—"

Matthew called down from the nav deck. "Commander Conrad, permission requested to report singularity on surface of planet Zelos."

"Permission granted."

"Decision noted. Execution proceeds. A non-natural structure has been observed to exist on the northern coast of the continent designated as Eurasia. This structure is ovoid in shape and approximately six kilometres long and three kilometres wide at its widest point. It possesses an abundance of substructures. The structure appears to belong to the class or set known as cities. The substructures appear to belong to the class or set known as houses, or fabricated protection systems. At our rate of passage over dayside, the structure will remain visible for a further seven point five minutes. With magnification of one five zero on manual telescope, it is possible to observe that—"

"Terminate report," said Conrad. "Maintain focus at one five zero. Take pix. I'll be with you in twenty seconds. Out."

The three of them were on the nav deck in less than twenty seconds. Conrad peered through the telescope. He saw a city—a stone-built city, with roads leading out from it like strands from a spider's web. He let Lieutenant Smith use the 'scope while he gazed at the telepix Matthew had already taken. Then Kwango looked through the 'scope. He let out a low whistle. At that moment, the *Santa Maria* passed from dayside to nightside, where there were no continents, only numerous archipelagos and a great ocean.

"So, Kwango, there ain't no people! 'Have some more booze, and stop worrying,' the man said. How do you feel now, you big stupid nigger?"

Kwango shrugged. "I feel like a small stupid nigger— white trash, sir! The probe surveyed this planet and it reported that—"

"God rot the probe! Haven't you learned not to put your faith in machines? And you, Lieutenant! Take it easy, you said. You are going to regret that remark because, for starters, I want the rest of the team out of the cooler, fast. So you and Matthew can get into top gear, as of now."

"Commander," retorted Lieutenant Smith icily, "it is my professional opinion that you could use a needleful of tranquilizer. What is the emergency? That city—if it is a city—has probably been there quite a long time. Why the hurry. It will stay until we come."

"Why the hurry, you stupid bitch?" roared Conrad. "Because I'm clearing for action, that's why! That city—and it damn well *is* a city—means people. They may have reached a technological level or they may not. But I'm not gambling. We'd look pretty bloody silly if they gave us a big hello in the form of a nuclear warhead."

"Commander," said Kwango patiently, "the probe did not register any radio emission or conventional use of energy. Nor did it register any sign of atomics."

"My God, I'm dealing with idiots!" exploded Conrad. "The bloody probe didn't even notice the city. Hasn't it occurred to you that its telemetry could have been all to hell?"

"More likely, Commander, sir," said Kwango, "that it orbited Zelos during a period of heavy cloud formations. It would still have been able to record radio emission, atomics, or industrial pollution, but it could not have seen the city."

"Black man, you picked the wrong time to be clever. You will stay on the nav deck and do the repeat telemetry yourself. When we go dayside once more, which is in about two hours, you will focus every kind of electronic eye we have on that city. You will also study the environs and extrapolate on probable flora and fauna, and you will make an assessment of the probable culture level we are likely to encounter when we touch down. So stuff that in your high I.Q. and make something of it. Because if you goof, bright boy, I'll have your guts for a necktie."

Kwango opened his mouth to speak, then thought better of it.

It was Matthew who broke the silence. "Commander," he said gravely, "I have interpreted the present situation as a period of stress. Is this correct?"

"It is correct."

"Then, sir, I am empowered to remind you that you are a real mean bastard. I trust this has a beneficial effect."

There was a brief silence. Conrad looked as if he had reached ignition point. He gazed at Kwango and slowly raised his prosthetic arm.

Kwango's expression was comic. His eyes rolled and an expression of utter despair spread over his broad, black face.

"O.K., Boss," he said. "So my time has come. Do I get a last request?"

"Request for a last request denied," grated Conrad. "For you, death is the easy way out. Get to work! You are going to regret the unfortunate accident of being born."

Indira could not contain herself any longer. She observed the woebegone expression on Kwango's face and then savoured Conrad's utterly ferocious look.

She dissolved into laughter. "Stop it," she pleaded. "Both of you, stop it! You're killing me."

Matthew said, "Query: Was the effect beneficial, Commander?"

Conrad said, "The effect was—" and then he caught Indira's look. And lost his control. A great grin spread over his face. "The effect was catastrophic, Matthew. . . . No, cancel statement. The effect was beneficial."

"Decision noted, Commander," said Matthew imperturbably. "Execution proceeds."

"God bless you, Massa Boss," said Kwango. "I allus knew you was de true white man."

Then they all fell about, laughing.

Conrad was the first to recover himself. "O.K. The party is over," he said. "Indira, Kurt, let's get moving. I don't like what we've seen down there. Suddenly, we have problems."

21

Phase Three

WE WON'T HAVE TO WORRY, WE'LL BE DEAD

Conrad had assembled his team in the saloon. Before he spoke, he inspected his new members objectively. Jane Ustinov was the last one to come out of the cooler. She still looked a bit grey and shaky, but Lieutenant Smith reported that she was in good physical condition, and had just eaten an enormous meal.

Conrad remembered her performance on the training programme. She had looked frail then, her abnormally pale face framed by long, black hair. But she was a remarkably tough young woman. She had given Kwango a few interesting surprises during the unarmed combat sessions.

Hal Mencken seemed to be in very good condition. But then he always did. He was a big man—bigger than Conrad and more muscular than Kwango—with a shock of curly, golden hair. It was incongruous. His features looked as if they had been sandblasted out of granite.

Hildegarde Dolfuss, the blond, bosomy Viennese woman, seemed to be on top of the world—which, in a literal sense, she was, since the *Santa Maria* was now orbiting Zelos at an altitude of one thousand kilometres. The first things one ever noticed about her, thought Conrad, were her breasts. Large, firm, challenging, inviting. He hoped that their existence would not adversely effect the Zelos mission.

Jean-Pierre Gautier was the really interesting one. Tall, slender, wiry. He looked like an athlete—a runner, or a jumper, perhaps. He was handsome in a typically French way. He was, as a rule, not very talkative. Back on Terra, the psych boys had classified him as an introvert.

Having surveyed the new Expendables, Conrad glanced

at Lieutenant Smith and Kwango. Both looked very tired, as well they might be. Indira had been heavily involved in the crash programme of resuscitation for about thirty hours—with, maybe an hour or two's rest while Matthew dealt with routine preliminaries. Kwango had been on duty on the nav deck for about the same amount of time. Besides supervising the detail-scanning of Zelos, he had helped Conrad to rig the radar and telemetry system to a direct control unit on the vessel's planetary drive. If anything lifted off Zelos, the *Santa Maria* would automatically take evasive action until Conrad reached the override controls on the nav deck.

As matters now stood, the *Santa Maria* was as ready as it could be for nasty surprises. Matthew was on the nav deck, standing watch; Mark was in the engine room, checking all propulsion systems; Luke and John were adjusting the recycling plant to the fact that seven human beings were now using oxygen, creating carbon dioxide, consuming food, excreting, and urinating; and Peter and Paul were checking out the emergency escape module and the life-support systems of the space suits.

Conrad was alternately proud of and infuriated by his robots. Because they were only complicated machines, they were stupid. Because they were very efficient machines, they were reliable. And, when the occasion required it, they were fast—very fast. Someone back on Terra had tried to fast-talk him into using so-called superior models, capable of evaluating a situation and taking independent action. The notion had filled him with horror. He didn't want any bloody robot making up its own "mind" what to do. Decisions were his province. All he wanted from his robots was total efficiency. With Matthew and the others of the S.P.9 series, he got it.

Now that he had mentally reviewed the condition of his entire team, Conrad was ready to advise them. He decided to keep it short and to the point. No propaganda about how important it was to prove Zelos for the benefit of mankind. It would be embarrassing if Indira and Kwango drifted off to sleep.

He cleared his throat. "This is the first occasion on which we have all assembled together in Zelos orbit.

Ustinov, you were the last out. How are you feeling?"

"I feel fine, Commander. I'm ashamed to admit it after such a terrific meal, but I'm still hungry. May I continue eating?"

Conrad smiled. "You may. One of the characteristics of emerging from S.A. is that the subject has abnormal hunger. Don't worry, Jane. We have all gorged ourselves. Hit the cheese board—that Stilton is perfectly ripe—unless you want one of the robots to programme another steak."

Jane Ustinov said, "The cheese is fine. There is only about half a kilo left. I hope nobody else wants any."

"Baby, we acknowledge your priority claim," said Hal Mencken.

"While Ustinov is catching up on time lost," went on Conrad, "I will summarize our present situation. As you know, more than four-fifths of the surface of Zelos is covered by water. There is a large number of archipelagos and islands, but only one continental land mass, which we have called Eurasia. If we can prove Zelos, Kwango estimates that ultimately it could support at least two thousand million people. So we are playing for big stakes.

"However, there is, as you know, a problem. We have discovered the existence of what is demonstrably a city. Further search has revealed similar but much smaller structures in nearby regions. How the robot probe missed these things, we do not know. Maybe the weather was bad during its orbital survey, maybe its circuitry was faulty.

"Anyway, the point is academic. Because of the encouraging data the probe brought back to Terra, we are now here. It took an awful lot of skill, energy and resources to get us to Zelos, and I don't intend to see all that effort wasted.

"The question is—are there people down there? Let us be clear in what we mean by the term 'people.' People are intelligent, tool-using animals who fabricate things they need. Other animals simply adapt to their environment. People are different. They also adapt to their environment, but they also change their environment to suit their own needs. I would remind you that people are not, necessarily, just creatures like us. They don't have to be humanoid.

"But we have to get down there and find out about them. Personally, I'm hoping they don't exist. We still can't find any traces of technological development. It's quite possible that the city is all that remains of a civilization that perished thousands of years ago. If that is the case, we only have the normal hazards of planet-proving." Conrad gave a thin smile. "Which, as Lieutenant Smith and Mr. Kwango will tell you, are practically a joyride."

"Commander," said Hildegarde Dolfuss, "what happens if we do find people—intelligent, tool-using animals as defined? Do we pull out?"

Conrad shrugged. "The decision isn't mine. I shall transmit relevant data back to Terra and let U.N. work it out. But if there are lots of people down there, I think we will have to terminate this mission. We are not empowered to take over planets where alien civilizations flourish.

However, this has yet to be proved. In view of the evidence at present available, it seems probable that Zelos is a big catacomb. But, in case it isn't, we have to be at the peak of physical and mental condition before we touch down. I am planning to set the *Santa Maria* down approximately one hundred kilometres south of the city, now designated as Enigma, after ten more orbits. That is in a little more than twenty hours S.E.T. Get some rest. Then get your muscles back into shape. If there are people down there, they are going to get curious when we make sonic booms in their sky. They may become resentful. We must establish a secure bridgehead in case they decide to get tough. Any questions?"

"Yes, boss." It was Kwango who spoke. "What if they are smarter than we are?"

"In that case, Kwango," said Conrad tranquilly, "we won't have to worry at all. We'll be dead."

Phase Four

TOUCHDOWN

The *Santa Maria*'s engines died. There was a brief silence. Conrad lay back on his contour berth and relaxed. So did Lieutenant Smith and Kwango. Conrad winked.

The rest unfastened their straps and hurried out of their contour berths. Hildegarde Dolfuss was the first to stand up. She uttered a little squeal and fell flat on her face. So did Jean-Pierre Gautier. Hal Mencken managed to stay up, but he was swaying like a drunken man. Jane Ustinov registered it all and lay back patiently.

Conrad said, "Now you know how much your muscles were weakened by S.A. and the time we spent in Zero G." He began to get out of his berth in a leisurely fashion. "Take it very slowly, folks, until your brains and muscles know they now have to work under G-stress once more. That way, you won't break any legs or arms. I hope."

He stood up and stretched. Slowly. Hildegarde Dolfuss, having gotten herself into a sitting position, regarded him with awe.

"Ideally," said Conrad, "I would have liked us all to stay in the ship for three Z-days, taking work-outs in the gym. But we don't have the time. We made one hell of a bang when we hit the sky of Zelos, and if anybody is at home, they'll know they have visitors. If they have sophisticated weaponry—which doesn't seem too probable —we are in trouble.

"Therefore, priority one is to ensure that the *Santa Maria* is ready for immediate lift-off. That is my province. Priority two is to get the external checks done as quickly as possible. A couple of robots are already assembling their sampling and testing gear in the air lock. I think Matthew has assigned Peter and Paul to the task. He is familiar, of course, with all touchdown routines. Priority three is to make ourselves secure from surprise and/or attack. We will establish external vid cameras hooked up to the command screens on the nav deck. As soon as possible after that we will unship two exoskeletons and construct a defence perimeter." He grinned. "After that, we'll get on with the hard work."

A robot's voice came over the intercom. "Paul reporting from air lock, Commander. Survey equipment ready and checked."

"Proceed through air lock, release ladder, transfer equipment dirtside. Inspect landing torus for possible damage and report back. Determine ship's attitude and report back. If no damage, and if attitude lies within acceptable parameter, you will proceed as follows: one, you will set up four semirotating vid cameras north, south, east, west at one hundred metres from vessel, and test hook-in to command screens; two, you will collect samples and return these to air lock; three, you will sweep an area of one thousand metres radius from vessel. If any hostile life form is encountered, you will return at speed without accepting any risks. Execute."

"Decisions noted, Commander. Execution proceeds."

Hildegarde Dolfuss had picked herself up off the deck. So had Jean-Pierre Gautier. Jane Ustinov was cautiously getting out of her contour berth, and Hal Mencken was taking a few exploratory steps.

"You'll all be operational in a few more minutes," he assured them. "Let's take a look at Zelos." He pressed a stud on the command console. A screen rolled back to reveal the observation panel. Because the *Santa Maria* was ninety metres high, it was impossible to look straight down. But the landscape beyond a hundred metres from the torus was visible.

Conrad had timed touchdown to take place just after daybreak. Now, with a reddish sun just clear of the horizon, the world outside was a world of dewy freshness and long shadows. The *Santa Maria* had come to rest on a great stretch of sparse grassland with, here and there, patches of shrubs and a few small trees. In the distance, to the planetary west, there was a range of rocky mountains, their peaks still shrouded in mist. To the east, there was forest. To the north, the grassland undulated and was lost over the horizon. Far to the south, there was the beginning of what looked to be desert country.

"It reminds me a little of the northeastern part of Spain," said Jane Ustinov. "Those mountains are so like the Pyrenees."

"Well, it sure is nice country," said Hal Mencken. "Looks like a man could enjoy himself out there."

"If it has any people, let's hope they are nice, too," observed Conrad drily. "Otherwise, Mencken, you won't have much time for the wonders of nature. . . . Now, let's get the immediate programme in shape. As soon as the samples are back in the air lock, Dolfuss, you will get moving on analysis. The first thing I want to know is if there is anything at all in the air that could be harmful to us. Ustinov can assist you.

"Meanwhile, Mencken will check the exoskeleton components and get two of them ready for taking dirtside. I want those exos operational at the earliest possible time. Matthew will assign a couple of robots to help you, Hal. Then, assuming Dolfuss reports favourably on the organic content of the air, you and Kwango and as many robots as can be spared will set up a temporary defence perimeter. Remember the gate must be wide enough to permit the passage of the hovercar. You can electrify, but don't feed into the system enough current to kill, just enough to deter.

"Gautier, check the efficiency and charge of the laser rifles. Then, after you have done that, I want you to design and plan for quantity production of a radio mine that can be buried outside the defence perimeter. Specifications are as follows: the mine must be as powerful as possible, bearing in mind the following limitations: one, it must be unaffected by heat, cold, pressure, but it must contain a circuit that will cause it to respond to pressure if triggered by a radio signal; two, it must be possible to detonate each radio mine independently without causing adjacent mines to explode—assuming the mines will be put down ten metres apart; three, a portable control must be constructed that will enable the operator to detonate individual mines at will, or switch to pressure control . . . Can you do this?"

Jean-Pierre Gautier shrugged. "You require a very sophisticated system, Commander. But, yes, this can be accomplished. It will, of course, take time."

"How long?"

"I do not know. I need time to think this thing out. Also, Commander, I shall require the use of robots for fabrication and assembly. Also, you will understand, I do not wish to commence such operations on board the *Santa Maria*."

"Yes, yes, I know all that," snapped Conrad impatiently. "As soon as we have a defence perimeter, we will set up an external workshop. All being well, you will have three robots assigned to the project. I want a hundred of those mines fast. How long, man?"

"Three, perhaps four, days I think."

"Make it two days, Gautier. Sleep loses valuable time. Lieutenant Smith will shoot you full of something to keep you awake."

Jean-Pierre Gautier smiled. "You are a hard man, Commander."

"I was hoping you'd notice."

Matthew came to the nav deck. "Permission to report, Commander?"

"Permission granted."

"Decision noted. Execution proceeds. The landing torus has suffered minimal damage. Repair priority low. Lift-off would not be affected. Vessel's attitude is three point seven five degrees from vertical. Lift-off would not be affected. Air, soil, and vegetation samples have now been deposited in air lock. Vid cameras have been set up and should be hooked in to command screens in seven minutes, plus or minus ten per cent. No significant local life forms yet encountered. Report ends."

"Good. You and I together, Matthew, will now check the propulsion systems. Kwango, you will remain on the nav deck and watch the command screens. If you see any fairies, call me."

"Yes, suh, Massa Boss."

"Lieutenant Smith, you will assume temporary command while Matthew and I inspect the chemical, thermo-nuclear and gravimagnetic systems. Check all operations. . . . Dolfuss and Ustinov, your samples are available. Get moving! Mencken, see to the exos. Gautier, what's keeping you? O.K., everyone, let's get the show on the road. If Zelos has any nasty surprises, we are damn well going to be ready for them!"

Phase Five

INDIGENE!

Before the end of the first Z-day, much was accomplished, and a startling discovery was made.

Dolfuss and Ustinov had found no nasty microorgan-isms or harmful spores in the air. The air consisted of a slightly richer oxygen-nitrogen mix than that of Earth. Its carbon-dioxide content was a little higher, but the trace gases were much the same, and it totally lacked pollutants. All in all, it was a healthy, invigorating atmosphere.

Conrad went dirtside as soon as he had checked the engines and had been given clearance by the lab. It was just before midday. The sun was warm, but not too warm. He sniffed the air appreciatively. It was a damn sight better than the air in the *Santa Maria*. It was *living* air.

Zelos, he thought, would be a very good place to give mankind another chance. If only there was not the com-plication of that bloody city a hundred kilometres to the north!

The air of Zelos was wonderful. It made the blood surge through his veins. It made his skin tingle. It even made him feel mildly optimistic. Maybe Enigma was a dead city. Maybe it was nothing more than an elaborate mausoleum—the last surviving gravestone of a vanished civilization. He hoped so. There would be no problem—ethical or physical—in taking over a planet that had once been the home of an extinct, intelligent race. But if a significant number of Zelosians were still around, there would be more than enough moral and practical problems to age him rapidly. For starters, the situation would have to be referred back to ExPEND and, ultimately, U.N. And while U.N. was busy debating the niceties of invading a world where people—defined as intelligent tool-using animals—were already in residence, Conrad and his team would have to sweat it out.

Well, if there were any surviving Zelosians, he would soon know. They could not have failed to register the arrival of the *Santa Maria*. The sonic booms must have been audible over half the continent. Maybe a reception committee was already on its way. The one consoling fact —if it was a fact—was that telemetry had not revealed any signs of atomics or technology.

Conrad took his mind from matters hypothetical and concentrated on matters immediate. Mencken had already gotten two exoskeletons dirtside and fully assembled. Kwango was now using one of them to help the robots set up the defence perimeter. At the present rate of progress, it looked as if the entire perimeter would be complete and hooked up to the *Santa Maria*'s generator well before nightfall.

Operating an exo, Kwango was a wonder to behold. He seemed to be totally at one with the anthropomorphic machine. Once harnessed into the control crown of an eight meters-high, atomically powered exoskeleton, Kwango could do the work of fifty men.

He held a bundle of angle girders in his exohand as if they were cocktail sticks. Every ten seconds or so, he methodically planted one firmly in the ground, and the robots fastened the wire mesh to it. The defence perimeter was going up at great speed—Kwango-style.

"That Kwango," said Hal Mencken, "he sure knows how to get the best out of these things. When he's operating, the darn machine looks as if it has come alive."

"It has," said Conrad. "Kwango has a lot of talent. The only trouble is, he knows it. From the way he's moving, Hal, I don't think he is going to need your help. I'll call him and find out." He took a transceiver out of his pocket. "Kurt, this is Conrad. Think you can do it alone?"

He heard Kwango laugh. "You seen me movin', Boss. Just keep out of my way, that's all. I wouldn't want to accidentally tread on you." To emphasize his point, he lifted one of the massive exolegs and stamped. The ground shook.

"Don't tread on any of the robots, either," snapped Conrad.

Kwango had the last word. His voice sounded shaky. "I wouldn't do that, Commander. Not even accidentally. They are my friends."

Conrad put the transceiver back in his pocket. "Your work is not wasted, Hal. I think we will need the other exos pretty soon. Get into this one and dump it fairly close to the section of perimeter defence that is already complete. When you have unharnessed, get another exo out, check that it is operational, and dump it likewise. After that, the priority is to get a workshop erected so that Gautier can go into production on his radio mines."

"You sound as if you are expecting real trouble, Commander."

"I'm not expecting anything except the unexpected," retorted Conrad. "I'm just taking out insurance. That way we live longer. If that city to the north is populated by nothing but ghosts, I'll break out a case of champagne. But if it contains people who don't take kindly to uninvited guests, we are going to be ready to defend ourselves."

"Aye, aye, sir."

"Also, I want the hovercar unshipped as soon as possible. I want to take a look around. How soon can you get it dirtside, bearing in mind the priorities of one more exo and the materials for Gautier's workshop?"

"Maybe three hours."

"Make it two. I want to take a good look around before the light dies."

"I'll try, Commander."

"Don't try. Succeed. That's what you're here for." Conrad took out his transceiver once more and called Lieutenant Smith on the nav deck of the *Santa Maria*.

32

"Conrad to Smith. Anything on the screens?"

"No, James. Nothing of significance. A few birds, that is all. No land creatures."

"Not surprising with the noise we made blasting down through the sky. Do the birds have any singular characteristics?"

"No, James. The nearest was at a range of about five hundred metres. It seemed a fairly ordinary kind of bird, but large—rather like a Terran eagle."

Conrad was suddenly irritated by her easy familiarity. "Lieutenant Smith," he snapped, "I must remind you that except for social and/or private occasions, you will address me as Commander or sir. Do you read me?"

There was a long pause. The voice that replied seemed to belong to a totally different woman. "I read you, sir. Over and out."

Conrad sighed. So much for Applecross and remembered intimacy. But the bloody woman ought to know his ways by now. Until Base One was secure, there was no time for anything but hard work and hard discipline. Conrad paced about moodily for a while, half registering Kwango's rapid progress and Mencken's work on the third exo.

Lying inert and unpowered on the ground, it looked like a slumbering eight-metre metal giant—which, in a sense, it was. But without a man or woman in the control harness, the exoskeleton was just useless junk. Robots could function independently, but an exo needed a human being harnessed into the control crown before it became alive.

Once the exo was activated, it was a formidable thing. It would amplify the strength of the human being by a factor of fifty or more. It would enable him or her to run at 70 k.p.h., pluck up trees as if they were flowers, dig ditches or do the work of cranes, excavators, bulldozers. Properly handled, the exos could be Conrad's Seventh U.S. Cavalry, a formidable force if the going got rough.

It was a consoling thought. As Conrad watched Mencken getting the third exo ready for operation, he began to feel a little more secure. The perimeter would be completed before nightfall, and three exos would be available for use. Not bad. With searchlights rigged and a robot monitoring the command screens on the nav deck, the team would be able to get a good night's sleep, free from fear of surprise attack.

The light was still good. The sky was clear. Darkness would not fall for an estimated four E-hours. Conrad called Matthew by transceiver.

"Conrad to Matthew. Have you any robots free for assignment?"

"Matthew to Commander Conrad. All robots currently employed. Mark and Luke are working with Mr. Kwango, this work being designated as priority; John is working with Mr. Gautier on components required for a proto-type radio mine; Peter is making adjustments to the re-cycling system, having been authorized to admit and filter external air; Paul is closing down non-essential engine room systems. I am scheduling discharge priori-ties."

"Mark and Luke must not be interrupted. Mr. Gautier has a time problem, so we will leave John with him. I want Peter and Paul to finish their work on fail-safe. Then have them assigned to Mr. Mencken. The discharge derrick is now free and I want the hovercar unshipped as soon as possible."

"Decision noted," said Matthew. "Execution proceeds. Estimated time for fail-safe termination is as follows—"

"Cut the crap," flashed Conrad, still irritable. "Over and out."

Matthew called back. "Query, Commander. Please define statement: 'Cut the crap.'"

"Cancel statement," snapped Conrad angrily.

Presently, the armoured hovercar was lowered dirtside. According to Matthew, all its systems had been checked while the *Santa Maria* was in orbit. But Conrad was not satisfied. He had Mencken give it another going-over as soon as it was on the ground. The atomic engine func-tioned perfectly, the main lift turbines purring like sleepy kittens. Mencken, being thorough, also checked shock absorbers, fuel feed, instruments and communications systems.

While all this was going on, Kwango had punched in the last of the defence perimeter supports. He left the robots to finish the wiring up and to hook in to the *Santa Maria*'s generator. When he had unharnessed, he came over to where Conrad stood.

"Going somewhere, Boss?"

Conrad ignored the question. "How much current are you going to put into the perimeter fence?"

Kwango laughed. "Enough to make a cow shit itself or to drop a man painfully on his backside. O.K.?"

"That's fine. . . . We still have some useful daylight left. I was thinking of making a short reconnaissance to the north. Ten kilometres or so. Nothing adventurous."

"You want company?"

"No. Until we have more data on this place, I don't want to risk more personnel than I have to. I expect to be away not more than an hour. If, by chance, I don't return, inform Lieutenant Smith that no search is to be carried out until tomorrow. Then, at first light, you unship the chopper and start looking for the bits. In the unlikely event of my non-return, it is my order that the *Santa Maria* will be kept on emergency lift-off readiness. Lieutenant Smith will retain command, but she will accept your advice. That is my decision. Want it in writing?"

Kwango shook his head. "Why don't you call de good Lieutenant and give her all dis info yourself?"

"I choose not to," said Conrad. "Now piss off."

Kwango raised an eyebrow, but he said nothing. He went aboard the *Santa Maria*. After all that work in the exo, he was feeling very hungry.

"Is the hovercar is good shape, Hal?" asked Conrad, turning to Mencken.

"Yes, Commander. All systems go. You got enough fuel for ten thousand kilometres without a recharge."

"I'm only going for a short trip. I'll be back long before the light goes."

Conrad got into the hovercar, settled himself comfortably, switched on the motors, and lifted. He cut in the thrust jet very gently and let the car glide very slowly through the gate-opening in the defence perimeter. Then he switched to high lift and swung north at 20 k.p.h.

After about one and a half kilometres he glanced back at the *Santa Maria*. It seemed absurdly insignificant—a slender, metallic column glinting in the yellow sunlight. Yet it was the home of seven people whose intention was to claim Zelos for mankind. He looked ahead at the rolling grassland that stretched to the distant horizon, and was instantly aware of the hugeness of the planet. That the *Santa Maria*, a tiny needle planted on the skin of such a vast ball of matter, could materially change the planet's entire future was a crazy notion . . -. Well, mankind specialized in crazy notions. And that tiny space needle with its biocargo had already claimed two planets. Miracles were not yet obsolete.

Lieutenant Smith called him. "*Santa Maria* to hovercar. Do you read me."

"I read you."

"Kwango has just told me about your sortie. Please don't go too far, Commander. And please don't take any risks. Over."

Her voice was still cold, but Conrad registered that she had used the word please twice. It was as good as an apology.

"Your requests are noted, Lieutenant. I intend to proceed north for about ten kilometres and reconnoitre. I will not take unnecessary risks, being a devout coward. Over and out."

Conrad was glad that she had called him. It was a kind of moral victory.

He accelerated to 50 k.p.h. The hovercar pitched a little as it sped over the uneven terrain, but not enough to disturb him. He looked for signs of animal life. There was some, but not much.

A creature vaguely like a kangaroo bounded out of the hovercar's path at high speed on a zigzag pattern. He wondered if its meat would be suitable for human consumption, and thought of lasering it. But he decided not to. Dolfuss and Ustinov could make their own safari later. With a little bit of luck, they would probably find a variety of animal life that future colonists could eat.

The *Santa Maria* was now about five kilometres away. Glancing back, Conrad could still see it. Now it really did look like a tiny needle—carelessly dropped on a wide, wide world. Ahead, the landscape was changing. The hummocks were getting larger. In the hovercar, it was beginning to feel like an old-fashioned switchback ride.

Conrad slowed down to 35 k.p.h. He didn't like what the movement was doing to his stomach. Presently, he was over the bumpy ground and onto plain once more. Now there were large, scattered patches of trees ahead—miniature forests. He boosted to 60 k.p.h. and steered expertly over the clear ground.

The light was beginning to fade—more rapidly than Conrad had expected. Soon he would have to turn back and head south.

He felt disappointed, deflated. Apart from the kangaroo-type creature and a few birds, he had discovered very little. He realized that the sonic effect of the *Santa Maria*'s descent and touchdown must have scared the shit out of the wildlife over a large area. But he had hoped that, by now, a few more indigenous animals would have showed themselves.

Directly ahead was a very large area of woodland. He decided that it definitely would be defined as a forest. Since the light was now poor, he decided to go to the edge of the forest, then swing back.

He dropped down to 20 k.p.h. The hovercar ambled towards the trees.

Then Conrad got the shock of his life.

He saw a man.

Briefly.

The man stepped out of the tree cover and faced the hovercar.

He wielded a weapon—possibly an axe. He shook it at the hovercar in a vague, challenging gesture. Conrad saw that the man's mouth was working, and judged that he was uttering threats, imprecations, or whatever. He eased the hovercar forward, slowly. The man vanished into the forest.

The first thought that hit Conrad was that the man was demonstrably a man. A *human* being.

The second thought that hit him was that the man wore a winged helmet, carried a sword and shield and looked just like an old-time Viking.

The third thought that hit him was that he had better get back to the *Santa Maria* before the light went altogether.

It would have been interesting to go into the forest and try to find out if Vikings existed on Zelos.

But Conrad was aware of the precept that discretion is the better part of valour. He opted out.

He turned the hovercar, and headed back to the *Santa Maria*.

Phase Six

NOT A NIGHT FOR THE LADIES

Conrad saved his revelation until after dinner. All the Expendables were in the saloon. Gautier, who had been working very hard on the radio mine project, had asked for his meal to be sent down to the workshop. He was very surprised when Conrad requested his presence in the saloon. So was everyone else.

The perimeter fence was fully rigged and a gate had been set up. The whole system was now hooked into the *Santa Maria*'s generator through a step up transformer. The vid cameras were operating; a series of searchlights had been placed at regular intervals inside the perimeter; Matthew was on watch at the command screens on the nav deck; Mark was on stand-to in the engine room; Luke, John, Peter, and Paul were patrolling inside the perimeter armed with laser rifles. The robots had precise orders—they were only to observe, and to take no action at all unless the safety of the vessel was at risk. However, those instructions could be changed instantly by Matthew's command circuitry. Conrad felt that the vessel was reasonably secure. Lift-off could be achieved in two point five minutes from the word go.

He surveyed his fellow Expendables benignly. Dolfuss

and Ustinov looked tired. Well, they had done a hard day's work. Their interim report on the local biosystem was good. Lieutenant Smith looked tired also— but her fatigue was probably only psychological. All she had had to do was sit in the command chair and sweat. Kwango was in good shape. So was Mencken. Therefore, they could share the night watch.

Conrad poured himself another brandy. He sipped it, savoured it, then he spoke. "When we were in orbit and first discovered the existence of the city now designated as Enigma, I asked Mr. Kwango to look into his crystal ball and give me a report on the local ecosystem and the possible culture level of the indigenes, if any. At the present time, part of his report seems to be an excellent anticipation of the findings by Dolfuss and Ustinov. We have touched down on an E-type planet that is almost too good to be true.

"Then Mr. Kwango went on to point out that, since we have only discovered the existence of one primitive city on the continent designated as Eurasia, and since there was no evidence of technological development, two assumptions could be made. One: that an intelligent race had existed but no longer existed. Two: that its culture level at the point of extinction was low-medieval.

"It saddens me to have to tell you that Kurt was both right and wrong. He was right about the culture level. He was wrong about extinction. So now we have problems. Nasty problems."

All eyes were fixed on Conrad. He savoured a brief, childish pleasure.

"Don't make with the funnies, Boss," said Kwango. "We've all had a hard day."

"Try this joke for size, genius," snapped Conrad. "This afternoon, about ten or twelve kilometres to the north, I saw a *human* being—an *armed* human being. And how do you like that?"

Kwango's mouth fell open.

"You can't be serious!" said Indira.

"Can't I, Lieutenant? Listen to this." He described the encounter and gave as much detail as he could. Then he added grimly, "Anyone—and this means chiefly you,

Kwango—who makes funnies about hallucinations, tricks of light, defective eyesight, imagination, or booze-visions is in dead trouble. I saw exactly what I say I saw. He looked like a Caucasian male with long, blond hair flowing from under a metal helmet. He carried a battle-axe and a shield. He was taller than me, broader than me, and he looked like a real tough cookie. End of message."

There was a short silence.

"Commander," said Kwango humbly, "would you care to bounce your prosthetic arm off my stupid head?"

"No. I need you. When this mission is over, I'll take up the offer. Meanwhile, we work out immediate strategy." He grinned. "In a curious kind of way, I feel very relieved."

"Relieved, Commander?" It was Mencken speaking. "You have given us the bad news, what's the good news?"

Kwango had recovered himself. "The good Commander means, Hal, that if this guy is representative of his race, they got no atomics, no high explosives, no lasers, no nothing that is going to neutralize our sophisticated weaponry. In short, we can relax."

"Right again, Kwango," said Conrad. "Also wrong again. You are going to have to improve your batting average if you want to remain our number one bright boy. . . . We are seven. How many are they? If these people are a lot of small, disunited tribes we may not have too much trouble, but if they have some kind of centralized authority, and if this centralized authority decides to take us out, sheer weight of numbers would eventually tell, despite all our fancy hardware."

"Boss, I got bad news."

"What's that?"

"They got centralized authority."

"How do you know?"

Kwango grinned. "I am just about to improve my batting average. The city, boss. *One* city only. Historically, cities in our E-culture have always developed into control bases. They got one city—so it's a capital city. If there are tribes in the area, you can bet—"

"Spare me the details. I get the message. So, it looks

40

as if the humdrum routine of planet-taming is going to be livened up somewhat."

"Commander," said Hildegarde Dolfuss, "isn't there some kind of U.N. regulation that says we can't colonize worlds populated by intelligent beings?"

"There is," agreed Conrad. "It's a little more complicated than that, but substantially, you have it."

"Then why don't we pull out before the indigenes start getting nasty?" asked Jane Ustinov.

"Listen, Ustinov. Listen, everyone," said Conrad intensely. "I'm going to give you the commercial, as my friend Lou Andreas would have described it, only once. It cost one and a half billion solars to put us down on Zelos. That money, recycled into other projects, could have extended or improved the lives of thousands of people on Terra. We don't matter. We are scrap-heap material. But the project matters. I have seen one man. One man only. We have touched down on a vast continent—bigger than any continent on Earth—and it has yet to be established whether the local population runs into thousands, hundreds of thousands, or millions. If Zelos is heavily populated, then it is no place for us or for future colonists. But if there is only a small population, it may be that Zelos will profit by colonization, just as we will. This is a matter for our masters back home to decide—in due course, and in their greater wisdom. Meanwhile, we find out what the score is. And if some of us get chopped in the process, it doesn't matter too much . . . In any case, the fact that there are people here— defined now as beings similar in appearance to *homo sapiens*—adds to the importance of the mission. We have to find out about them. And the most important question of all is: why are they like us? So get it into your heads that though we, individually, are expendable, the mission is not."

Mencken said, "Why don't you toss the problem back to base, Commander, before the going gets rough?"

"Hal, you should know the energy cost for subspace transmission. We can only send for a few seconds at a time, otherwise the generators will burn out. And what the hell do I send? I have seen one angry Viking-type gentleman so may we come home, please? Not on your life! When I send, I send full data on Zelos. So, ladies and gents, the party is over. Now we get into overdrive. Tonight you will get a good night's sleep—with the sad exception of Gautier. No, cancel that. Kwango and Mencken will share watch on the nav deck. Matthew is already monitoring the screens, but I would like one of us to be with him. I don't expect trouble, but we must be prepared for it. Gautier, I no longer require a hundred radio mines."

"I am delighted, Commander. There is a design problem that—"

"No, Gautier, I want a thousand—fast."

"Mon dieu! It is not possible. We do not—"

"Make it possible. You can use all robots except Matthew, if need be—but only for daytime operation. Don't waste time, man! Get moving!"

With a dazed look on his face, Gautier left the saloon.

"Kwango, Mencken, get as much rest as you can. May I suggest four hours on, four hours off. That will give each of you some sleep worth having. You are going to need it. Kurt, remember the type of stockade we built for protection against the death worms?"

"Sure do, Commander. Good Kratos pine, sharpened ends, planted at an outward angle of sixty degrees, three metres high. How's that for total recall?"

"Not bad. Tomorrow, we do the same again—only twice as fast. Mencken will unship and ready more exos. I'll help and Lieutenant Smith will help, while Dolfuss and Ustinov mind the store. There is a forest three kilometres to the east. That is our nearest timber supply. At first light, we get out there. We can't rely only on an electrified fence any more. For all I know, those guys might not care how many of them get burned, so long as some get over."

Hildegarde Dolfuss said, "Commander, there is something you have overlooked."

Conrad gazed at her for a moment, then said, "Thanks. You're right. We unship the chopper before we take out more exos. Lieutenant Smith can use it to make a distance reconnaissance to the north. Then we don't get nasty surprises. I hope."

"I didn't mean that."

"Oh," He looked at her blankly. "What did you mean?"

Hildegarde's eyes sparkled. "This is the most exciting event in the whole of human history. If we can prove that there are people like us on a planet many light-years from the solar system, it will cause a revolution in the biological sciences back on Terra."

"Right now," said Conrad drily, "I am not interested in biological revolutions back on Terra. I am interested in survival."

Hildegarde either ignored or was unaware of the warning signs. "And if, by chance, we can get a specimen and test for genetic compatability we could—"

Conrad cut her short. "O.K. Dolfus, there's a way to speed up research. Just walk out of here, head north and wait until one of those characters hits you on the head, tears your trousers off and forces your legs open. That's the quick way to test for genetic compatability. But if that doesn't appeal too much, save your theorizing until we have time for it. Right now, survival takes precedence over science. Do you read me?"

Hildegarde Dolfuss resented being put down. "It appears," she said, "that coarseness and brutality take precedence over rational thought, Commander."

Conrad shrugged. "In my own feeble way, I try to be rational, Dolfuss. But I am also going to be coarse and brutal—if necessary—until this base is as secure as we can make it. Now shut up and take your heaving boobs to bed. You may not get much beauty sleep for a day or two."

Red-faced, Hildegarde Dolfuss left the saloon.

"Was that necessary, Commander?" asked Lieutenant Smith icily.

Conrad was tired. He knew he was tired, and he knew that he should not have fired both barrels at Dolfuss. But, what the hell? It had been a long day; and, from the looks of things, life was going to get harder, not easier.

"Lieutenant," said Conrad, with a cutting edge in his voice, "you should know better than to question my authority in the presence of others. When you signed ship's articles, you signed for loyalty and obedience to lawful commands. Your remark could be construed as lack of loyalty. I will overlook it on this occasion. Dismissed!"

Indira Smith stood up. Her eyes were blazing with anger. She looked, thought Conrad, very beautiful when she was angry. The luxuriant white hair framed her brown features perfectly. She was one hell of a woman.

He tried to think of a way of cooling the situation, but before he could do so, Lieutenant Smith gave an exaggerated and impudent salute and marched from the saloon.

There was a strained silence. Conrad scratched his silver patch irritably and poured himself another brandy. He did not look at the others. He did not want to see their faces. This is a hell of a way to get the show on the road, he thought dully. Tomorrow, I'm going to need a hundred and ten percent effort from those two bitches. But I've fouled it up. Black mark, Conrad! Is this the way to handle a crew? You stink!

It was Kwango who reduced the tension. "Commander, this is not your night for the ladies. All you got to do now is smash Ustinov; then we menfolk can share the rest of the brandy real democratic."

Conrad flashed Kwango a grateful glance. Then he looked at Jane Ustinov and saw that she was very pale.

"Don't worry, Jane, the storm has passed. You and Hildegarde did good work today. I see from your interim report that we don't have to worry too much about bugs . . . Do you think I overreacted?"

"Hildegarde was right, Commander," she said tensely.

"Right? Right about what?"

"We need a specimen. If we could study one of these people—even if only for a short time—we could find out a great deal. Maybe we could save ourselves a lot of trouble or conflict."

"She's right, Boss," said Kwango.

"O.K., she's right," conceded Conrad. "But priority one is still security. After that, we will try to collect, not a specimen, but a man or woman of this planet. People are

44

not specimens. People are people. We treat them as such." He laughed grimly. "With a lot of luck, they might treat us as people, too."

Phase Seven

MATTHEW STRIKES AGAIN

At first light, everyone ate a hasty but substantial breakfast and then moved into action. The atmosphere in the saloon was still highly charged. Hildegarde Dolfuss and Lieutenant Smith spoke only to Conrad when he spoke to them, their answers for the most part monosyllabic. He tried to make soothing noises. He asked them if they had slept well. The answer was yes—in both cases, though neither of them looked at all as if they had slept well. He solicited their opinions on the quality of robotic cooking. Lieutenant Smith defined it as adequate, Hildegarde Dolfuss defined it as reasonable. Conrad went through the whole gamut of safe topics—the weather (it was a fine, cloudless morning); the comfort and the discomfort of the *Santa Maria*'s living accommodations; the day's schedule of work; the programme for finding, analysing, and using local flora and fauna as food; and several other routine matters.

The responses he got were mechanical, terse and impersonal.

Finally, he lost his patience. "Hell and damnation!" he roared. "Don't you stupid females realize that I am holding out an olive branch? The last thing I need today is a couple of sulky women. Goddammit, grow up!"

Matthew had just entered the saloon. His robotic mind analysed the situation instantly.

"Commander, in the present circumstances I am empowered to remind you that you are a real mean bastard."

Kwango rolled his eyes, covered his face with his hands and was heard to mutter, "Oh, my Gawd!"

45

There was a silence.

Conrad scratched his silver eyepatch irritably. He tried to contain his anger. Finally, he said, "Kurt, enough is enough. You cancel that programme or I'll spread you very thinly over a large area of Zelos."

Matthew said, "Was my evaluation of a stress situation correct, Commander?"

Hildegarde Dolfuss giggled. Indira looked at Conrad with a faint smile. Hal Mencken stared at his breakfast plate with great concentration. Jane Ustinov choked somewhat on her coffee.

"It was, Matthew," Conrad managed to say. "Your timing was excellent." He caught Indira's glance. His anger evaporated. He grinned. "O.K. So I *am* a real mean bastard. But you have always known that, Lieutenant, haven't you?"

She nodded. "It was hardly a news flash." Her tone of voice told him that she was prepared to accept a truce.

He turned to Dolfuss. "I'm afraid I overreacted last night. O.K.?"

Hildegarde Dolfuss smiled. "O.K., Commander. You are the veteran, I am the amateur. I should have known better than to—"

"You had a valid point," he conceded. "We have to get to find out what these people are like as soon as possible. Meanwhile, the security of the base remains priority one. . . . Now, if you have all finished breakfast, let's go. What's the exo situation, Hal?"

Mencken said, "I got five unshipped, assembled, and tested. The chopper is also dirtside, checked and ready to lift."

Conrad raised an eyebrow.

"I put in a couple of hours before breakfast, Commander. It seemed like a good idea."

"It was a good idea, Hal. Do you want to catch up on some sleep before you join the rest of us?"

"No thanks. I'll do my sleeping when we are secure, like you said."

"Fine. So now we have more than enough exos ready. . . . Hildegarde, can you monitor the command screens and maintain contact with us poor labourers for about six to eight hours without being relieved?"

"No problem, Commander."

"Good. . . . Jane, I recall that you showed some talent on basic exo training. Would you care to join us? With five exos in action, we should have the stockade up before midday."

"My pleasure, Commander."

Conrad finished his coffee. "That's it then. All systems go."

The stockade was completed well before midday. Conrad was amazed at the speed with which the stripped and sharpened tree trunks were delivered and planted in position. The robots assigned to punching holes in the ground could hardly keep up with the supply of timber. Kwango, as always, was the outstanding performer. In his exo, he handled the six metre tree trunks effortlessly.

The stockade gateway was exactly opposite the gateway of the electrified perimeter defence. As he surveyed the entire structure, Conrad relaxed. The gateways, clearly, would be the weak points. They would have to be protected by some of Gautier's radio mines when they were ready.

He and a couple of robots were already beginning assembly operations in the duralumin hut that had been established near the electrified fence. Gautier had yet to carry out field tests on his half dozen prototypes, and doubtless, there would be modifications of one kind or another. But, when Conrad last talked to him, Gautier seemed confident that he would have the first mines rolling off the assembly line within another twenty-four hours. That wasn't bad.

Lieutenant Smith and Jane Ustinov had already unharnessed out of their exos and were now back aboard the *Santa Maria*. With a couple of robots to assist them, Kwango and Mencken were putting the finishing touches to the stockade. The robots, using rivet guns were wiring all the logs together. Mencken was systematically planting buttress logs and Kwango was constructing a double-thickness gate.

Conrad began to feel pleased. If there were any serious

conflict with the local population, he felt reasonably confident that the *Santa Maria* could lift off before both defence systems were breached.

He radioed Lieutenant Smith. "How are things topside, Lieutenant?"

"A few interesting items on the screens, Commander. The wildlife is beginning to move back. We registered a herd of quadruped herbivores a couple of kilometres to the north. About thirty. I took a look through the manual telescope. They resemble terrestrial deer. Dolfuss wants to go out and bag one. Over."

"We'll discuss that possibility at lunch. What else?"

"More birds of various shapes and sizes—alarmingly conventional in appearance and performance. So much so that they make me feel we never really left Terra, and it's all an elaborate hoax. Over."

"No hoax, Lieutenant. Zelos does begin to look like what the old fantasy writers used to call counter-Earth, but let's not get lulled into a sense of false security. What's for lunch?"

"The all-American beefburger, Kratos-style, with French fried, braised celery and *petit pois*. How does that grab you?"

Conrad laughed. "Your choice?"

"Yes."

"You are getting sentimental, Lieutenant. Lou Andreas died some time ago. But it's nice to think he left his mark."

"He was our brother, James."

"Yes, Indira, he was our brother. . . . Kwango and Mencken are finishing off. I'm going to talk to Gautier, then I'll come topside. Break out a litre of red. We'll drink a toast to Lou."

Gautier was ready to test his prototype. One of the robots buried the mine outside the stockade. Conrad was allowed the privilege of pressing the button, while Gautier operated the high-speed camera that would record the effects of the explosion. The resulting crater measured over three metres wide and nearly two metres deep. It made one hell of a bang.

Gautier channelled the results to the *Santa Maria*'s

computer for analysis. The computer agreed with his own subjective assessment. The mines could be detonated independently, without causing adjacent mines to explode. Hole in one. He was pleased. He was also red-eyed and very tired.

"O.K., Jean-Pierre, you have scored," said Conrad. "Congratulations. Come and have lunch."

Gautier was swaying. He was out on his feet. Conrad felt guilty. Gautier tried to pull himself together.

"But you said you wanted a thousand of these little toys very fast. I have no time for lunch. Perhaps you will have something sent down to me."

Conrad glanced at the stockade. Kwango, indefatigable, was still in his exo, carefully hanging the heavy gate.

"Jean-Pierre," said Conrad, "you need a couple of hours of relaxation. I think we can afford it. Now come to the saloon and get an all-American beefburger. That is an order. Can the robots go it alone from here on?"

"I think so, Commander."

"Good. Have them continue fabrication while you take it easy for a while."

After lunch, Conrad discussed the next phase with the team. "The *Santa Maria* is now reasonably safe. When Gautier has his mines planted, I don't think we need fear anything, except a sophisticated large-scale attack. You can have at least one more robot, Jeanne-Pierre. You can also have Hal if you think it will speed matters up."

"I would be grateful if Hal can be spared to help. Do you already have a site pattern for the minefield, Commander?"

"I've drawn a rough one—it's in my cabin. The thing can be varied according to your judgment. But I want the heaviest concentration in front of the gates. Hal, you O.K. for pitching in?"

"Glad to. I know some about laying minefields, Commander."

"Good. Now the rest of us are going to be busy also. I want someone to stay topside, keep an eye on the screens and maintain communications. That suit you, Jane?"

She shrugged. "If you say so, Commander. I'd rather take a stroll on Zelos."

"Your time will come. Someone has to mind the store. Hildegarde, I want you to explore our immediate environs. Take a robot, and take laser rifles. You are authorized to drop any specimens of animal life you see for analysis and study. You are not authorized to tangle with any human or humanoid beings. If any put in an appearance, you are to call Ustinov, inform her of the situation, and then fall back to the stockade with all possible speed. Understood?"

"Understood, Commander."

"Lieutenant Smith, I want you to take the chopper and make a reconnaissance over the city that we have designated Enigma. Take lots of pix. I don't think the people there will be able to throw much at you, so go in as low as possible at your discretion. I want as much data on that city as possible—but not at risk to yourself. If you see any significant movements of indigenes en route, report back to Ustinov, who will relay the information to me. O.K.?"

"O.K., Commander."

"What about me, Boss?" asked Kwango. "Are you forgetting your curly-haired black genius?"

"No, Kurt. You and I are going hunting. We'll take the hovercar. We are going to try to catch a Zelosian."

Stage Two

CONTACT

Phase One

BLOODBATH

Beside laser rifles, Conrad had taken a couple of anesthetic guns in the hovercar. He and Kwango were also wearing armorlite jackets. He had a nasty feeling that catching a Zelosian was going to be a tricky operation—with, possibly, some rather unwelcome consequences.

If, for example, the mission succeeded and word somehow got back to the city that a bunch of mechanized marauders from the south were taking liberties with the local population, it seemed most likely that there would be considerable resentment, perhaps enough to inspire the locals to attempt to take out the invaders.

It was a nasty dilemma.

Still, contact had to be established sooner or later. An evaluation had to be made sooner or later, and the data transmitted back to Terra. All this, sooner rather than later. Time was on the side of the indigenes, not the Expendables. From the slender evidence gained thus far, it appeared that the Zelosians did not have any fancy weapons they could use. But if there were enough of them, and if they could be mobilized to attack in a disciplined fashion, life at Base One could be made difficult and hazardous.

Conrad, at the controls of the hovercar, took roughly the same route that he had taken on the previous day. He took it more slowly, veering from side to side in a smooth steady zigzag. Kwango sat beside him, using binoculars.

The *Santa Maria* was now ten or more kilometres to the south.

"Boss," said Kwango, "I got a feeling that we are being watched."

"I have the same feeling, Kurt. So let's assume that we are being watched. These people can't be unaware of our arrival. If you were a tribal chief and something moving and spectacular came zooming down through your sky, what would you do?"

"I'd send out reconnaissance parties, and when they told me what the score was, I'd decide whether to get tough or send presents."

"I have a feeling that we are not going to get presents," said Conrad grimly. "The character I saw yesterday did not look friendly at all . . . We have passed about ten patches of woodland. I am willing to bet there were Zelosians in each of them."

"Let's test the theory, Boss. There is a nice stretch of forest a kilometre ahead. Why don't we roll up to it, ground, and play sitting duck?"

"O.K., Kurt. We'll test the theory. But only one of us will get out of the car—no matter what, if anything, happens to the other. We can't afford to lose two men and a valuable piece of equipment."

"I'd better be the decoy, Boss. Lieutenant Smith would laser me anyway if I hightailed back without you."

Conrad shook his head. "Kurt, to you, black is beautiful. It may not be so to these light-skinned Zelosians. They may be less axe-happy if they see someone who looks more like them."

Kwango snorted. "That's racist talk, Massa Boss."

"We live in an unfair world, Kurt. I'm going to set the car down over there, about fifty metres from the trees. We'll wait a while. Then, if nothing happens, I'll get out and take a look-see."

Conrad took the hovercar close to the trees, very gently, very slowly. He cut the engine. The machine settled.

Ustinov came in on the radio. "*Santa Maria* to car. Do you read me? Over."

"I read you. Over."

"Lieutenant Smith reports seeing several groups of indigenes between fifty and seventy kilometres north. Average group strength, about twenty. Most are armed—swords, axes, bows. Some are armoured, some are mounted. They ride shaggy, horned creatures that have the function of horses. Lieutenant Smith says they look like Texas longhorns in fur coats. Over."

Conrad gave a faint smile. Now what the devil would Indira know about Texas longhorns?

"Thank you. Nothing to report here. Over and out."

Kwango stared at the trees. "Can't see nothing, Boss, but I still got the feeling we are being watched."

Conrad reached for the anesthetic gun and checked that the magazine held its full twenty darts. He thought of taking a laser rifle also, then decided against it.

"Boss, I still think you ought to sit tight and let me wander about. I'm younger than you, faster than you, and more agile."

"So you are, Kurt," said Conrad tranquilly. "But I'm the man who makes the decisions. . . . Leave the door open and cover with a laser rifle. I'll stay in sight, and I'll stay close. Don't start burning unless you think I'm in real trouble . . . Conrad paused. "What a pleasant afternoon. We ought to be sitting in deck chairs, drinking lager and watching cricket. Then, carefully, he eased himself out of the hovercar.

Kwango grinned, reached for a laser rifle, checked its power. "What-ho, old chap. Now I know what made de British Empire great."

Conrad took a good look around. He could see nothing but trees, grass, blue sky. No birds, no game. Nothing. The sun was warm. There wasn't even a whisper of breeze to distract him. The world of Zelos was eerily quiet.

They are there, he told himself. I know they are bloody there. Slowly he walked towards the trees.

The first Zelosian stepped out of cover.

He was a magnificent specimen. He was more than two metres tall. Long blond hair flowed from under his winged helmet. He carried a metal shield on his left arm. His right hand held the end of the long haft of a double-edged battle-axe, the head of which rested on the ground by his feet. His chest was bare, and he wore leather trews. He gazed at Conrad fearlessly.

Then the second Zelosian came out from the trees. He was similar in appearance, except that he carried a long, heavy sword.

Neither made a sound. They just stood there, waiting, about twenty metres away, watching Conrad impassively.

He moved slowly, very slowly, towards them. They just stood still and relaxed.

Kwango called, "It's like shooting fish in a barrel, Commander. Drop them both, then we can pick up the bits and go home and relax."

"Before Conrad could reply, the Zelosians lifted their weapons and uttered bloodcurdling battle cries. The ground began to shake.

A troop of longhorns—perhaps ten—each mounted by an armed warrior, hurtled out of the forest like guided missiles. And they all seemed to be aimed at Conrad.

The time for contemplation was over. He dropped the first three with his anagun, hitting the beasts, not the riders. Two warriors struggled clear, the third lay groaning with his leg trapped under the unconscious animal. Conrad felt two blows, and glanced in amazement at a couple of arrows lodged in his armorlite jacket.

The rest of the troop came on. The leader held a three metre lance, aimed unerringly at Conrad's chest.

Kwango burned off the arm holding the lance. The warrior didn't seem to care or notice. He just came on. Conrad dropped the warrior's longhorn. Then he pumped an anesthetic dart into the man on the ground. It seemed kind. Pretty soon he was going to feel a lot of pain.

The rest of the riders wheeled sharply and melted back into the forest. Those shaggy longhorns—or whatever they were—could move and maneuver with speed and precision, Conrad noted.

He had no time for further contemplation. The two foot soldiers and the two dismounted warriors came at him, shouting like madmen.

He managed to drop one almost immediately, burying the blade of his axe in the soft ground. As Conrad aimed at the other one, another arrow hit his armorlite jacket, knocking him sideways. His shot missed. The warrior came on. Another arrow ricocheted off his prosthetic arm, and again he missed. Things were not looking too good, he thought vaguely. If the rest of them stayed in the tree cover and popped away with their bows, sooner or later one of them would get him in the leg or even in the head.

"Hit the deck!" roared Kwango. "I'll burn him!"

But it was too late for that.

The warrior was already upon Conrad. He knocked the anesthetic gun away with his shield, and raised his sword for a massive chop that would split Conrad's skull as if it were an apple.

As the sword came down, Conrad's prosthetic arm shot out with fantastic speed. His fingers grabbed the wrist of the Zelosian. The movement of the sword was halted, as if it had hit a block of concrete.

The Zelosian stared at him in amazement.

Conrad swung the wrist to one side, tightened his grip, felt bones break. The sword dropped harmlessly from the crippled hand.

With merciless efficiency, Conrad twisted the crushed wrist and threw the Zelosian to the ground. There was no time to look for the anagun. He leaped on the warrior and chopped at his throat. The man grunted, gurgled, twitched, lay still.

Before Conrad could get to his feet, the mounted Zelosians had regrouped in the forest and were coming at him again. Sensibly he stayed down.

From the hovercar, Kwango used his laser rifle with devastating effect.

Conrad glanced up and counted seven riders, variously armed. Kwango lasered the shaggy longhorns first—hoping, doubtless, to limit the bloodbath.

All but one of the riders managed to struggle clear of their dead mounts. They came on.

Conrad found his anagun. He dropped two. But Kwango had to burn the remaining five. He didn't have enough time merely to disable them. He had to sweep the entire group. They screamed and died.

The stench of burned flesh drifted over Conrad. He vomited. Presently, he recovered himself and stood up.

"You O.K., Boss?" called Kwango.

"I'm O.K."

"Then get back here fast. I'll laser anything that moves."

Conrad made it back to the hovercar.

No arrows came from the forest. There was nothing but a deathly silence.

Conrad flopped into a passenger seat and slammed the door. "Some party," he said shakily.

Kwango opened the medical kit and found the brandy. "Boss, you just have a natural talent for disaster. Now drink this before you say another word."

Meekly, Conrad obeyed. The brandy tasted dreadful, but it settled his stomach. He looked through the windscreen at the dead and unconscious Zelosians. It was one hell of a scene of carnage.

"I've messed it up," he said at last.

Kwango smiled. "You are alive and uninjured, Commander. And we got ourselves a choice of several sleeping Zelosians. What's the problem?"

Conrad sighed. "Massacre is the problem." He gestured towards the bodies on the grass. "When word of this gets back to the city, whatever their culture level, they are going to consider us to be a bunch of homicidal psychopaths."

Kwango shrugged. "They just kept on coming, Commander. What else could we do? These characters are death or glory merchants."

"That is what bothers me," said Conrad. "They don't count the cost." He sighed. "Well, the damage is done. Let's pick up one that is still alive and in good condition and get back to the *Santa Maria*. We'll take the youngest looking. In theory, the younger a person is, the less rigid his attitudes are. Having gone to all this trouble, we don't want to wind up with a case of culture shock."

"You think it's safe for us both to leave the car, Boss?"

"Probably not. You go and inspect the damage. I'll cover you while I call Ustinov and give her the score."

The youngest looking Zelosian was one of the mounted warriors whom Conrad had managed to anesthetize. By Terran standards, he looked to be eighteen or nineteen. No one shot at Kwango or came out of the forest. Maybe they had had enough. Or maybe they were all accounted for.

By the time Kwango brought his burden back to

the hovercar, Conrad had radioed the *Santa Maria*, and two robots were already at work constructing a prison-cage for the Zelosian in the defence perimeter.

Kwango dumped the unconscious Zelosian in the back of the hovercar, and wiped the sweat from his forehead.

"Hot work, Boss. This character has to weigh in at about ninety kilos."

"Hot work, indeed," agreed Conrad. "Has he got any broken bones?"

"None that I could feel. I expect de good Lieutenant will want to take a look. . . . How long does the anesthetic last?"

"Three to four hours. We have plenty of time."

"Boss, I been thinking. Some of those guys out there don't look too good. The living, I mean. There's a guy with a broken leg, and there is the one whose wrist you crushed, and there's the one whose arm I burned off, and there are a couple of others with broken legs. If they get no attention, they are going to be in pretty poor shape."

"I take your point. Let's get moving with the medical kit. I'll hit them with painkillers and antibiotics, you do what you can with splints, bandages and the aerosol sealer." He laughed grimly. "I don't think they will want to write thank you letters when they come round. But it may dawn on them that we don't just destroy for kicks."

Phase Two

WE KILLED TOO MANY ZELOSIANS

Back at the stockade, Conrad discovered that the day had gone well for everyone.

Hildegarde Dolfuss had bagged a fair amount of wild-life—the small creatures she had anesthetized and caged, the large ones she had killed. She had collected several small herbivores—one looked oddly like a small, terrestrial badger, and another had something in common with the hare. She also had several of one species that was obviously very common. They looked grotesquely like a hybrid of guinea pig and otter. There were only two samples of big game, but they were impressive. One had some resemblance to a roe deer, and the other was a shaggy longhorn—the apparent Zelosian equivalent of a horse.

Gautier and Mencken had not been idle. The ground outside the stockade gate had now been extensively mined. They hoped to complete the rest of the minefield in about four more days.

Lieutenant Smith had some very interesting pictures, not only of the city, taken at low level, but also of its occupants and of the entire route north.

But the prize trophy was the unconscious Zelosian brought back in the hovercar.

As the sun began to sink towards the horizon, Kwango took the limp body out of the hovercar and laid it gently on the ground.

The Expendables gazed at it in wonder.

"Commander," said Hal Mencken, "you weren't kidding. This guy looks like he walked right out of Terran history, about a thousand years back."

"He *is* human!" explained Dolfuss triumphantly. "I'll run tests, of course, but I'm betting he is genetically compatible. When we get back to Terra, this is going to rock the whole of biological science to its very foundation."

"*If* we get back to Terra," said Conrad drily. "Kwango and I have just indulged in a massacre. We didn't plan it that way. But that's what happened. Something tells me there may be a return match."

Lieutenant Smith said, "Is he wounded?"

Conrad shrugged. "I don't think we broke anything. He is going to come round pretty soon. What are your recommendations, Lieutenant?"

Indira glanced at the cage that was nearing completion. It looked like a large rabbit hutch—one half consisting of a pen with duralumin bars, and the other half consisting of walled night quarters.

"He is not ready for that thing," she said decisively.

"Even if he is uninjured and in the best of health, the traumatic experience he has just been through could produce serious physical and mental complications."

"I'm not having him aboard the *Santa Maria*," snapped Conrad. "Not unless he is nailed down. These people play rough and they don't count the cost."

"I'll nail him down," said Indira. "I'll knock him out for the night and I'll pump him full of tranquilizers. When he wakes, he will be as docile as a kitten."

"You guarantee that?"

"Yes, I guarantee it."

"O.K., Lieutenant. He is your responsibility." Conrad rubbed his forehead wearily. "Well, it's been a long hard day. Let's go clean up and eat something. You can give me your reports over dinner. Now that we have the stockade and the gate section of the minefield operational, I think we can all get a good night's sleep. Matthew can watch the screens, and we'll have all available robots patrolling. . . . Where are you going to put our unconscious friend, Lieutenant?"

"In the sick bay."

"Then strap him down to the bed good and hard— just in case he doesn't react to your needle-juice like you think he should."

Conrad was dead tired. He promised himself the luxury of a bath and an early night. He hoped Matthew wouldn't have to call him out.

Dinner in the saloon began as a noisy affair, with everyone apparently trying to talk at once. Conrad let the babel continue while he ate his main course. It was roast lamb, brussel sprouts, new potatoes. Matthew —the impeccable Matthew—had even programmed the mint sauce the way Conrad liked it, with sugar and black pepper.

Conrad ate with relish and reverence. He had a proper respect for Terran food. It was a link across the light-years. Soon the Expendables would have to live on whatever delicacies Zelos had to offer. That was an essential part of the mission. There was no point in attempting to colonize if you couldn't live off the land. But for a couple more days, perhaps—until Dolfuss had discovered what local food could be eaten—there remained the immense luxury of Terran meat, Terran fish, Terran vegetables.

He ate the last scrap of food from his plate and gazed at his companions with disapproval. Most of them were letting the delicious meal grow cold. They lacked a proper sense of proportion. They would pay for it.

"Now shut up, everyone!" he said irritably.

The babel ceased. Everyone gazed at him. The robot Paul took away his empty plate. Conrad glanced briefly at the robot's control dome. He thought he detected a knowing look, a faint smile. Imagination. No lips, no eyes. Only vision circuitry, sense circuitry and sound circuitry.

He gazed disapprovingly at Lieutenant Smith. She had barely touched her food. Dammit, she was a veteran. She should know better.

"Well, Lieutenant, I am ready for your report."

"Yes, Commander. Do you want to see the pix first?" She produced a large bundle of photographs.

"I'll look at them when I have finished my meal. Right now, all I want is significant data. Proceed."

"Low-level reconnaissance yielded the following results: estimated population of the city, ten thousand, plus or minus fifteen percent. No significant technology apparent. There was panic in the streets when I went low. My altitude was about two hundred metres. A number of bowmen tried to hit the chopper, but gravity was not on their side. These people are skilled metal workers; they have the use of fire, the wheel, the lever. They understand the basic principles of mechanics. I saw various wheeled vehicles. The layout of the city is more formal and more sophisticated than I expected. Some of the large central buildings are made of stone, but away from the city centre, the buildings are relatively small and mostly made of wood. The city wall is made of stone. It is only about two and a half-to-three metres high. It was obviously constructed originally for defence, but it certainly was not manned. A river runs through the city and down to the sea, about three kilometres to the north. The river is bridged in various places and it powers a number of water wheels, but I couldn't discover what their function was. That's about all, I think. Doubtless more will be revealed when the pix are studied in detail."

"Thank you, Lieutenant. You had better continue—or rather start—your meal now," said Conrad maliciously. "It may be getting cold."

Indira glanced at her plate and saw globules of fat congealing on the roast lamb. She was about to push the plate away.

Conrad sensed the anticipated movement. "I hope you will eat it all," he said. "The people of Terra paid thousands of solars to put that delicious meat on your plate so many light-years from home. It would be interesting to calculate how many Indian children could have been saved from death by starvation for the same amount of money."

"Commander, I will enjoy the meal all the more," said Indira with irony in her voice, "for being reminded of its high value." She began to tackle the cold lamb, the cold sprouts, and the cold potatoes with ferocious dedication.

Conrad put the rest of his Expendables through the same mangle—Gautier and Mencken, then Dolfuss and Ustinov. Kwango observed the operation with some amusement. He had caught on quite early. His plate was as clean as Conrad's.

"Now we'll all get sensible," said Conrad finally, as he sipped his coffee. "First, we are all going to get a good night's sleep—I hope. Lieutenant Smith is temporarily responsible for our captured Zelosian. Tomorrow she will bring him back to the land of the living. Dolfus, if you want sections of his tissue for analysis, you had better take them while he is out cold." He grinned. "I presume you would also like samples of his semen. If so, don't tell me how you propose to obtain them, because I don't want to know . . . At first light, Lieutenant Smith, I want you to get our young alien friend conscious and in full possession of his faculties. I want him to talk."

"But we don't know his language," protested Jane Ustinov.

"That is why I want him to talk. Kwango, you will tape his utterances. If he doesn't utter, persuade him, coax

him, kick him. Run his vocabulary through the computer.
I want the English equivalents by midday."

Kwango was shaken. "Boss, semantics is a complicated
science."

"So simplify it. That is what you are hired for. You are
the bright boy in our midst. Justify your reputation. I
want to be able to talk to that bastard and/or his friends
very fast. Get the basic vocabulary and grammar structure,
then systematize it for easy assimilation. Understood?"

Kwango shrugged. "O.K., Boss. But you are breaking
the rules of the game." He glanced significantly at his
clean plate.

Conrad flushed angrily, and scratched his silver patch.
Blast Kwango! Blast him for being right!

"You are lucky I haven't already broken a few other
things, joker," he said, referring obliquely to the insert
in Matthew's programme. Finally, he turned on Hildegarde Dolfuss once more. "Dolfuss, before you start inves-
tigating genetic compatability and other lofty patterns,
perhaps you would bring your great mind to bear on more
immediate problems. You have your animal specimens. I
want to know what we can eat and what we can't, pretty
damn fast. . . . Now, everyone, please do continue to
enjoy this simple Terran style meal. It will be something
to remember when you are gorging yourselves on Zelosian delicacies."

He stood up, flung his napkin on the table, and strode
from the saloon.

There was a silence.

No one ate.

Presently, Mencken said, "What has gotten into the
old man? Why did he lose his cool?"

"Hal," said Kwango gently, "dat 'old man' throws a
very long shadow when de going gets rough. Humour him.
He may have only one good eye and one good arm, but
humour him."

"What the hell is this all about?" demanded Jane
Ustinov.

Kwango gave her a fond gaze. "Jane, you are a lovely
girl, but stupid. We killed too many Zelosians. That is
what it's all about."

Phase Three

KWANGO'S FANDANGO

Lieutenant Smith had given the young Zelosian a thorough examination. While he was unconscious he had been stripped, X rayed and monitored on the electrocardiograph, the electroencephalograph and the electromyograph. Blood samples had been taken, as well as tiny sections of tissue.

The results of this comprehensive investigation indicated that, in all significant respects, the Zelosian was a normal human being, which was totally amazing. The only variation from the human norm was that his skeletal system was rather large, and his muscles correspondingly strong. He would have compared favourably with an Olympic athlete.

Hildegarde Dolfuss obtained her semen sample by a simple method that had been used more for pleasure than for scientific investigation by men and women for untold centuries. Triumphantly, she took the blood, tissue and semen samples for analysis.

She was like a child with a plethora of Christmas presents. She didn't know which to tackle first. Whatever the final results, as she told Lieutenant Smith, conventional evolutionary theory would have to be completely reexamined.

Meanwhile, with the aid of the robot Mark, the Zelosian was restored to his clothes, his light armour and his dignity.

Kwango came to collect him. While he was still unconscious, he was transferred to the pen that had been built inside the defence perimeter. Armed with a tape recorder, Kwango went into the pen with him. Lieutenant Smith gave the Zelosian a mild stimulant—enough to bring him to consciousness, but not enough, she thought to neutralize the tranquilizer. Kwango sent a robot for food and drink. Lieutenant Smith had recommended only well-cooked steak and water. There could be little doubt that the Zelosians were meat eaters; and water would be the safest drink to give him.

About an hour after daybreak, the Zelosian uttered a great sigh, opened his eyes and sat up. He gazed at Kwango, shook his head violently, then looked again. He obviously didn't like what he saw. He groaned, closed his eyes, sank back and retreated into the foetal position.

Kwango kicked him—gently.

"Listen, old sport," said Kwango in an atrocious imitation of the ancient Oxford accent, "I, too, have a sensitive psyche. I know just how you feel. For me, black is beautiful and white is a big mistake on the part of the Creator. You have it reversed. So we start equal. Now kindly sit up and have your breakfast, there's a good lad."

Kwango kicked him again—with a little more force.

The Zelosian sat up, opened his eyes, closed them, rubbed them, opened them again.

"That's my boy." said Kwango encouragingly. "Now eat your breakfast, son. We got a hard time ahead."

The Zelosian took the plateful of steak, sniffed at it cautiously, then tore off a small fragment of meat with his fingers. He touched it with his tongue and savoured the taste. Then he put it in his mouth and started to chew.

Kwango smiled encouragingly. The boy swallowed the morsel. Then he attacked the rest of the meat ravenously. Ignoring the knife and fork that had been provided, he held the steak in his hands and bit off large gobbets. He chewed and swallowed with remarkable rapidity. Kwango gazed at him with approval.

The Zelosian shook his head once or twice and blinked. Then he took the plastic beaker of water, dipped his finger in it and then licked the finger experimentally. Apparently satisfied that the water was only water, he drained the beaker in a single swallow. Then he stood up, flexed his muscles, and broke wind.

"Nice manners, son," said Kwango. "Now please say something." He switched the recorder on and placed it in a corner of the pen.

Kwango was a big well-built man, but the young Zelosian had an even more powerful build. He gazed at Kwango warily.

It was a fine morning. The sun had been up less than an hour, but already the day promised to be warm.

Conrad, having finished his breakfast, came dirtside. He strolled over to the pen, tested the strength of the bars with his prosthetic hand, and spoke to Kwango.

"How goes it, Kurt? You got anything out of him?"

"Not yet, Boss. He's eaten, he's had a drink. Now we go to work."

"Don't waste time. We need a vocabulary . . . Incidentally, Lieutenant Smith says he's got everything we have—only more so. And Dolfuss swears she could get herself pregnant by him."

Kwango grinned. "I'd like to see her try."

"She still sees this mission as a ticket to a Nobel Prize," said Conrad drily. "She seems to forget that Stockholm is twenty-four light-years away."

The Zelosian was shaking his head some more, and blinking. He still looked a bit dazed. Maybe he was still feeling the effect of the knockout shots. Kwango turned away from him for a moment to say something to Conrad.

That was a grievous mistake.

The Zelosian lunged, grabbed his shoulder and spun him round. A massive fist struck his chest. Before he slammed against the bars of the pen and slid painfully down to the ground, Kwango had time to realize that the young man had been aiming at his heart.

Some joker!

Kwango sat on the ground, trying to get his breath, trying not to groan. He saw stars—little bright points of light, floating from all directions over his blurred vision.

He expected two events: one, that the Zelosian would now put the boot in while he was helpless; two, that Conrad would enter the pen and neutralize his opponent.

Neither event happened. Kwango was confused.

His vision cleared. There was still pain in his chest, but he could breathe. He saw that the Zelosian was waiting for him to get up. Then he heard Conrad's voice.

"This is your party, Kurt. Enjoy it."

"Thanks, Boss," he groaned. "Friendship is a wonderful thing."

Kwango got to his feet. The Zelosian came at him. This time he tried for a bearhug—apparently, he disapproved of the fact that Kwango was still able to breathe.

He got the bear hug and began to squeeze all the air out of Kwango's lungs. But he didn't like what he got from Kwango in return.

Before he became entirely breathless, Kwango managed to clap his hands loudly, behind the Zelosian's head. Kwango has stiffened both arms.

His stiffened biceps connected with the young man's ears, simultaneously. The warrior grunted with pain and immediately released the bear hug. Then, to show his appreciation of the treatment, he slammed a massive fist into Kwango's belly.

The black man went down again, coughing, gasping.

"Interesting," observed Conrad. "I must tell Lieutenant Smith that these people don't react too well to tranquilizers. Pick yourself up, Kurt. The gentleman is waiting."

"Boss," gasped Kwango, "you are a hard man."

"So is this character. But, at least, he plays by Queensberry rules."

Kwango tried a flying head butt from the ground. It connected to the solar plexus.

The Zelosian went down with a surprised look on his face.

"Score one," said Conrad. "Kurt, this is developing into a propaganda exercise. You have to smash him by yourself. Then, when we send him back to his people—"

Kwango did not look at Conrad. He kept his eyes on the Zelosian. "Boss, I never knew propaganda could be so painful."

Conrad laughed. "We learn something new every day."

The young man had picked himself up. He smiled at Kwango, and held out a hand.

"Friends?" said Kwango hopefully. He took the proffered hand. Another big mistake.

He was whipped into a high somersault and landed flat on his back. Painfully.

Kwango groaned. Every bone in his body hurt.

The Zelosian laughed.

Conrad said, "I think you are making progress, Kurt. You have established basic communication. Our young friend is feeling happier."

"*I* am not feeling happier," said Kwango. "This is going to have to be done the hard way."

"I want that vocabulary, black man, and I want it fast."

"You'll get it, white trash, sir."

Kwango picked himself up. He looked groggy. He swayed slightly and rolled his eyes. Conrad gazed at him with disapproval. Oddly enough, the Zelosian backed away as far as he could. Two seconds later, Kwango discovered why he had backed away, as the boy suddenly rushed forward with a tremendous body charge that could not be checked.

Kwango turned sideways as if to meet the charge with his shoulder. Then, with expert timing he bent double. The Zelosian hurtled over his back just as Kwango straightened it. The young man rose more than two metres into the air, somersaulted and came down flat. The force of his fall shook the ground.

He lay twitching, unconscious, for a few moments. Then he recovered his wits and staggered to his feet.

"Score two," said Conrad. "For a while you had me worried."

Kwango smiled. He had got his breath back. "Stay for the fancy work, Boss. You could learn something."

He smiled at the Zelosian who was still dazed, moved swiftly towards him, then expertly turned and delivered a mule kick to the young man's jaw. He went down again.

"Score three," said Conrad. "My faith in you is returning, Kurt."

Kwango said nothing. He waited patiently till the Zelosian had gotten to his feet once more. Then he reached out a hand and gripped the young man on each side of his jaw. The fingers tightened. A nerve hold. The Zelosian was powerless.

"Note the artistry, Boss," said Kwango. "This guy is

not going to say thank-you for what he is about to receive."

Expertly, Kwango delivered a head butt. The apex of
his head hit the centre of the Zelosian's forehead.

The young man's knees buckled, his eyes closed and he
fell in a heap.

"Here endeth the first lesson," said Kwango.

"Score four. Now that you have had your fun, will you
kindly stop bullying the boy and get on with the job?"

Temporarily, Kwango was speechless.

The young Zelosian sat up but did not attempt to stand.
He rubbed his forehead gently. He looked up at Kwango
with some respect.

Kwango tapped his own head and grinned. "I ain't got
no headache, boy. Now stand up and get sensible. There's
work to do." He gestured with both hands. The Zelosian
seemed to catch on. He stood up.

Then he spoke. He pointed to Kwango and said, *"Dees
pirsh yu daritza."*

Kwango nodded approvingly. "I like that, sonny. Keep
at it."

The Zelosian pointed to himself. *"Yos pir yu daritza."*
He stepped forward and held out his right hand—palm
uppermost, as if to show that there was nothing hidden.

It didn't look like a trick. Kwango emulated the gesture.

The Zelosian held out his other hand similarly. Kwango
followed.

Slowly, the Zelosian turned the palm of his left hand
down. Intuitively, Kwango realized it was some form of
greeting or acknowledgement. He, too, held out both
hands and turned the palm of his right hand down.

The Zelosian came closer. He placed his upturned hand
under Kwango's downturned hand, and his other hand
over Kwango's other hand.

"Daritza smern. Yos paluri."

"Daritza smern," repeated Kwango. *"Yos paluri."*

It was pure luck, as he discovered later, that he had
said exactly the right thing.

"Very moving," observed Conrad drily. "I'll leave you
with your new playmate, Kurt. I'm going to take the
chopper and have a look at the scene of yesterday's

debacle. I'll take Lieutenant Smith, in case any of the wounded need further treatment. Get some sense out of this boy and report to me at lunch."

Phase Four

CONRAD GETS CARELESS

Conrad had to check twice that he had found the right patch of forest. All that remained of yesterday's fracas were a couple of dead longhorns. He circled low over the trees to see if there were any Zelosians in concealment. The foliage was dense and he could see only a few small patches of clear ground. Hundreds of Zelosians could be hidden below, and he would not be able to detect any trace.

During the short lift from the stockade, Lieutenant Smith had maintained a stony silence. Doubtless she was still smarting from last night's treatment at dinner.

"I'm going down to treetop level," he said. "See if you can spot any movement. If there are any characters down there mounted on longhorns, maybe the air blast and the noise of the motors will make the animals panic."

Dutifully, Lieutenant Smith peered through the binoculars.

Conrad radioed the *Santa Maria*. "How are things back at the ranch?"

"Fine, Commander," said Jane Ustinov. "Jean-Pierre and Hal are making great progress with the rest of the minefield. They are using Luke and John. They think they will have the north section completed before the end of the day. Hildegarde is hard at work in the lab, with Matthew assisting. She says you can have longhorn steak whenever you want to try it. High protein, almost no fat. I haven't heard from Kurt, but Hal went to see how he was getting on. He reported that the prisoner was talking quite a lot and that Kurt had apparently mastered the use of some Zelosian words."

"Good. . . . Did Dolfuss say what longhorn steak tasted like?"

"A little strong—rather like venison."

"We'll get used to it."

"Commander, I'm bored. I have square eyes from watching the screens. I'm a marinologist, remember?"

Conrad gave a grim laugh. "Ustinov, I think there will presently come a time when you will look back fondly on the periods when you were bored. I haven't forgotten that you are a marinologist. There is a lot of ocean for you to go at on this planet. Just be patient. If the local boys don't take us out, or force us to abort the mission, you'll get your chance. Over and out."

Lieutenant Smith put the binoculars down. "Nothing to report, Commander."

"O.K. We'll go down and take a look dirtside."

Conrad set the chopper down about a hundred metres from the trees. He put on an armorlite jacket and reached for a laser rifle. "Cover me. I'm going to take a look at the scene of the crime. There may be something of interest left behind . . . These people must have a pretty good communication system. They take their dead and wounded away rather smartly."

"Commander," said Lieutenant Smith, "would it not be more logical for me to take a look?"

"Why?"

"I have tin legs. I can run four times faster than you."

"A valid point," conceded Conrad. "So put on a jacket, take a laser and keep your head low. I'll keep the vanes moving and I'll cover you. These Zelosians are good with the bow, and they attack at speed and without thought for the cost."

Lieutenant Smith got out of the chopper and walked cautiously towards the dead longhorns. Conrad kept the door of the chopper open, and rested the laser rifle on his knees. He gazed intently at the ragged line of trees. There was no sign of movement. Maybe Zelosians were there, maybe not. Maybe they had developed a healthy respect for laser power—though he doubted it. They hadn't

71

seemed the kind of people who would lose their nerve.

Lieutenant Smith was inspecting the dead longhorns. She put down her laser rifle—which was a stupid thing to do—and then she pulled something out of the hide of one of the dead beasts. It looked like a dagger. She lifted something from the carcass. It looked like a tattered piece of fabric. Finally, she picked up her laser rifle and came back to the chopper.

Conrad kept his eyes on the tree line.

"One of those beasts had a broken neck," she said. "It must have happened when you dropped it. The other had a broken leg. Somebody put it out of its misery by cutting its throat." She held out the bloodstained dagger and a large piece of cured skin. "This was pinned to the body. It looks interesting."

Conrad took the strip of parchment and studied it. There was a kind of writing upon it. Six lines of symbols had been skilfully painted or drawn. The symbols reminded him of an ancient style of writing he had once seen on Earth. He dredged his memory. Cuneiform! This was the language used in the ancient inscriptions of Persia and Assyria.

The mystery deepened. Human beings on Zelos who had developed a cuneiform style of writing. Dolfuss was right. The clever boys back on Terra were in for a few nasty surprises.

Conrad handed the strip of parchment back to Lieutenant Smith. "Maybe Kwango can do something with this. If he can get a vocabulary out of that young Zelosian and then get the boy to read the parchment, we might get somewhere . . . This thing is obviously some kind of message to us. It may be very important."

"Why does it have to be a message to us?"

"They took away their dead and wounded," he explained patiently. "They took everything except the dead longhorns. They guessed we would come back, so they left the parchment."

"Couldn't it be a message to others of their own kind? Something like—Don't tangle with the strangers because they have formidable weapons?"

"It could," he admitted, "but I don't think so. My guess

is that when the patrol—or whatever—that we took out didn't return to base, another patrol was sent to look for them. They didn't like what they found. So, properly enraged, they left this note. Most likely it says they are going to smash us for being naughty. Or it could even be an invitation to some kind of parley. Anyway, I think it is significant. . . . Sorry I brought you out unnecessarily, Indira. Shall we improve the shining hour by taking a look farther north?"

"I would prefer to go back to base," said Indira evenly. "There is a lot of lab work to be done. Hildegarde Dolfuss will need as much help as she can get."

"About last night," he began in a conciliatory voice.

"What about last night, sir?" She gazed at him coldly.

"Nothing. Cancel statement. I'll drop you back at the ship, then I'll head north myself."

"Thank you, Commander. If we survive Zelos—or to be more optimistic, when we have proved Zelos—I shall apply for a transfer from your team."

"Fine," said Conrad grimly. "I will recommend it. I will also recommend you for a command of your own. It's about the worst thing I could wish on you."

Lieutenant Smith said nothing.

Conrad lifted the chopper and turned south. Ten minutes later, he touched down inside the defence perimeter.

"Give the parchment and my compliments to Kwango," he called as she stepped out of the chopper. "Tell him to make his playmate sing loud and clear. Communication is now top priority. I'm going to take a look at the city. If I am not back in two hours, abort this mission and return to Terra."

"Why?" Indira was surprised.

"Because, Lieutenant," said Conrad with some malice, "you do not yet have sufficient maturity to deal with nasty situations. When you get your first command, I only hope the planet you have to prove is as docile as Kew Gardens."

He lifted before she was clear of the vanes, and was gratified to see her white hair streaming in the down current.

of animals were grazing. But whether they were wild or domestic animals, he had no means of knowing. There did not appear to be any people about—unless they had taken cover at the sound of the chopper—so probably the animals were wild. It looked as if any future colonists would have a good supply of meat.

Far to the right, Conrad noticed what looked like a village or town. It was about ten kilometres away. He decided to investigate. It would take no more than a few minutes. He checked that the automatic camera was locked in position and had a full magazine. Then he swung the chopper to the right.

He went in low—far too low, as he realized a few moments too late. He had wanted to take close range, detailed pix of the people, their houses, the lay out of the village, and any kind of machinery or conveyances that they might have.

Overconfidence was his undoing. He knew he was safe from arrows and such. But the occupants of the village did possess one kind of machine that he did not expect. They had a kind of ballista, or catapult. He made one low pass over the village, observing the houses and the people who came out to stare at him. He was struck by their apparent lack of fear. They did not scurry for cover as a primitive race might when confronted by some noisy, inexplicable contraption that could fly through the air.

They stood and stared. Those with bows loosed off an arrow or two. Conrad smiled. Arrows—even if they managed to hit—were not going to do the chopper any harm.

His first pass was made at one hundred metres altitude. He pressed the camera stud repeatedly and got lots of good pix. His second pass was lower—fifty metres altitude. More good pix. High definition.

On his third run, he went in at thirty metres. And they were ready for him.

He saw the ballista too late. Somehow, they had managed to elevate the machine. The wooden throwing arm came up and a sizeable chunk of stone was hurled at the chopper.

It was a lucky shot. A fantastically lucky shot.

The missile whanged off the blades, and then the chopper began to shake.

Conrad fought for control. He lifted. Somehow, he managed to get the machine up to a thousand metres. He turned and headed south. But the dreadful vibrations told him he was not going to make it back to base.

He radioed. "Chopper to *Santa Maria*, do you read me? Over!"

There was silence.

The chopper was now losing altitude and the vibrations were increasing. He tried again. "Chopper to *Santa Maria*, do you read me? Over."

"I read you, Commander," said Ustinov. "It's close to lunch time. Will you be back soon or shall we keep your meal heated?"

"Toss it in the garbage can," snapped Conrad. "I've goofed. I'm about seventy kilometres north, the chopper is damaged and I'll have to come down soon. Lieutenant Smith had orders to abort the mission if I did not return in two hours. Tape this: Current orders to abort cancelled. Mission only to be aborted if commander does not return in forty-eight hours E-time. Conrad. Have you taped?"

Ustinov sounded very agitated. "Message taped, sir. Kurt, Hal and Jean-Pierre can come out in exos to get you and the chopper. Shall I—"

Conrad cut her short. "No one is to come out to get me. Security of the *Santa Maria* remains priority one. I'll get as far south as I can before the bloody machine falls apart. Then, hopefully, I'll make it on foot. Over and out."

Conrad fought for control of the chopper, but he was fighting a losing battle. No matter what he did, the machine now continued to lose altitude and the vibrations got worse.

"Damnation!" he said. It looked as if he were going to have to ground about seven or eight kilometres south of the village.

He was down to four hundred metres now, and making no more than ninety k.p.h. The chopper felt as if it were going to fall apart at any moment.

He concentrated. He concentrated on getting every kilometre out of it that he could.

When he finally hit dirt, he found that he had done better than he had dared hope. He had managed to put about eleven kilometres between himself and the village. He came down close to a small patch of trees. He had chosen the spot intentionally. It occurred to him that some bright native might guess that the lucky ballista shot had done for the sky machine. In which case, there could be a pursuit. In which case, he was in trouble.

Conrad killed the motors and wiped the sweat from his forehead. Now he would have to move quickly in case a posse of irate Zelosians was already heading south.

He radioed the *Santa Maria*. "I'm down safely. I'm now less than sixty kilometres from base. It is my intention to abandon the chopper and start marching."

It was Lieutenant Smith who answered him. Her voice was full of anxiety. "How did it happen, Commander?"

He thought he might as well confess his idiocy and get it over with. "I went in too low over a village. They had a machine that chucks rocks. One lucky shot got the vanes. I ought to be court-martialled."

Indira said gently, "You are not injured?"

"I would have reported it if I were," he snapped irritably.

"Let me send Kwango in an exo. He'll lift you out in no time."

"No. You have my orders. I don't want the Zelosians to know about exos yet. I'll call if I really need help. Over and out."

"Good luck, James. Over and out."

He did not waste time reprimanding her for calling him James. He slipped a pack of food concentrate into one of his coverall pockets, made sure that he had his personal transceiver, slung a one litre water canteen over his shoulder, and checked that his laser rifle was fully charged.

The chopper contained a variety of emergency supplies. There was a large med kit and two small ones, there were two more water canteens, and a couple of laser rifles. There was also an assortment of food packs, a variety of knives, some small tools and a hatchet. He considered his supplies for a moment or two. He thought about taking extra water and food, but they would become a weight problem. Finally, he selected the smallest med kit and a serviceable sheath knife that could be strapped round his waist.

He got out of the chopper and looked with some mortification at the damaged blade. It was a bloody miracle that it had not sheared.

He turned towards the nearest trees and started to laser off some of the lower branches that were well covered with leaves. Hastily, he stacked the branches around the chopper. It wasn't much of a job of camouflage, but it was better than nothing. There was no easy way of screening the vanes. But Conrad estimated that if no one passed nearer than five hundred metres, the chopper would remain invisible. Anyway, it was the best he could do.

He checked his equipment, then turned south and began to march.

Phase Five

MANHUNT

The day was warm, but not unpleasantly so. If it stayed fine and dry—and from his brief experience of Zelosian weather it looked as if it might—the march back should not present too many problems. The ground was not too rough, there were no steep hills, and the grass varied from ankle height to knee height. Under such conditions, Conrad thought he could average six kilometres an hour, Z-time.

The Zelosian day was twenty-six hours, twelve minutes E-time. When the *Santa Maria* had touched down, personal timepieces had been adjusted for convenience to a twenty-four Z-hour basis, though the starship's chronometers maintained standard E-time. The Expendables had experienced little difficulty in adjusting to the Z-hour which, after all, was only five and a half minutes longer than the E-hour.

Conrad glanced at the electrochron. It was almost fourteen-thirty—which reminded him that it was long past lunch time, and that he ought to feel hungry. He didn't. But he found a patch of ground on a slight rise and allowed himself ten minutes to sit down, chew some food concentrate, and swallow a few mouthfuls of water.

He sat facing north, scanning the horizon for signs of pursuit, and calculating how long it would take him to get back to the *Santa Maria*. If he could keep up six k.p.h. it would take ten hours. But, even though he was very fit, he knew he could not cover sixty kilometres without breaks.

Mentally, he divided the march into four two and a half hour stints, each of the first three stints to be followed by a half hour of rest. So, allowing for no complications, the journey ought to take about eleven and a half hours. Therefore E.T.A. would be approximately 2 A.M. tomorrow.

Allowing for no complications! Aye, there was the rub! Weather conditions could change, the night could become too dark and cloudy for him to check his direction, there could be Zelosians between him and the *Santa Maria*, or a pursuit party could catch up with him.

As he chewed the food concentrate and looked north for signs of pursuit, Conrad suddenly realized that he had forgotten to take two useful items of equipment from the chopper—the binoculars and the atomic torch.

He scratched his silver eyepatch irritably and swore. Then he reminded himself that anger at his own stupidity was profitless. The binoculars would have been useful, but the atomic torch was no great loss. When darkness came, he would only have to switch to infrared vision. However, that would slow him down somewhat. Despite his intensive training, it took much longer for his brain to interpret infrared vision than for normal vision. He hoped devoutly that it would be a clear, moonlit night.

The ten minutes were up. He took a final look north,

in the direction of the village, saw nothing that indicated pursuit, and began the long march back to the *Santa Maria*. He had been walking steadily for about three hours, glancing regularly over his shoulder, when he noticed a herd of grazing animals about two kilometres ahead. As he came closer, he saw that they were shaggy longhorns. He got to within about five hundred metres of the herd and stopped. He estimated that the herd was about two hundred strong.

Now he had a problem. Were they domesticated creatures or wild? And in either case, how would they react to an intruder on foot? If they followed the pattern of certain wild herd animals on Earth, it might be that bulls, or stallions, or whatever, were stationed strategically to protect the group from attack. In which case, they might resent Conrad's presence and try to do something about it. He could laser a few bulls if he had to, but if that action provoked a stampede, there was no way of calculating what would happen. It would be impossible to laser the entire herd if they stampeded in his direction, and Conrad did not want the success or failure of the Zelos mission to depend on whether or not he was stamped into the ground by a herd of terrified animals.

Reluctantly, he decided that he had better make a wide detour. He licked his finger and held it up. The light breeze was southerly. Rapidly, he calculated that it was going to cost him an extra three kilometres to get clear of the herd.

Looking at the lie of the land, he judged it best to make the detour on the western side of the herd. As he turned, he glanced back—and saw riders less than two kilometres behind him, galloping at high speed.

Were they tracking him, or were they coming to round up the herd? A good question, but unanswerable. Lack of sufficient data, as Matthew would say.

The grass where he stood was fairly high. He dropped flat instantly, then raised his head to see how many riders there were. He counted seven, and they were coming on fast.

The sixty-four thousand solar question now was—had they actually seen him? He had not been on a skyline, so they could not have seen him in silhouette. His coverall was not so different in colour from the colour of the grass that it would stand out. But sunlight might have glinted on the metal of the laser rifle or other items of equipment.

- Still, there was nothing he could do about it. There was no place to go, nowhere except the grass in which to hide. So, plan 13Z—which, in spacemen's idiom meant: there is nothing constructive you can do, so wait and see what happens.

He did not doubt his ability to take out seven mounted Zelosians with the laser rifle. But more carnage was the last thing he wanted. Sooner or later, he wanted to establish a peaceful relationship with the people of Zelos. A lot of dead bodies wasn't going to help that aim.

He decided that he could just afford to wait until they were about two hundred metres away before he started burning. Those longhorns could move fast, and if the riders fanned out, he would have problems.

Raising his head cautiously, he saw that they had pulled out about five hundred metres away. They did not seem interested at all in the herd. They were peering about in all directions.

That told him what they were looking for. They were looking for the cretinous character who had buzzed their village. And, since they were looking on the ground and not at the sky, the inference had to be that they had already found the chopper.

The riders fanned out, but not with any great urgency. Therefore they must still be unaware of his presence.

Flies winged noisily round Conrad's head. One settled on the tip of his nose and made him sneeze. He cursed silently. Then he relaxed. The sound of a sneeze was not going to carry five hundred metres.

Presently, one of the riders pointed. He had seen something to the east—some kind of unidentified movement, presumably. He took off in pursuit. The rest of the riders wheeled and followed him.

Conrad wiped the sweat from his forehead. He waited until the Zelosians were about two kilometres away, then he stood up and began to make a detour to the west, round the herd of longhorns.

He made up for lost time by cancelling his next rest period. Instead of sitting down and relaxing briefly, he swallowed a couple of pep pills. No doubt he would pay for the double dose later with a blinding headache, and aches and pains throughout his overworked limbs. But the important thing was to get back to base at top speed.

The sun was getting low in the sky. Conrad glanced at his electrochron. Darkness would descend in little more than two hours. He quickened his pace. He wanted to cover as much ground as possible before he switched to infrared vision.

In the twilight, a predator came at him. It came out of nowhere with a fantastic leap. It must have been stalking him. He managed to laser it before it connected—but only just. The creature fell dead at his feet. The smell of burning flesh made him sick. When he had recovered, he forced himself to inspect the animal—what was left of it. The head had been burned off, but the body seemed to have all the grace and power of a puma.

He marched on through the twilight, irritated because he would soon have to switch to infrared, but relieved also that the Zelosian's chances of overtaking him would be greatly reduced when darkness fell.

It was then that he heard a strange sound. At first, he could not identify it, though it was familiar. For a few seconds, his mind refused to accept the reality, preferring to believe in an illusion.

But the sound became louder, and reality could not be avoided.

He heard the baying of hounds.

Phase Six

THE HOUND OF THE BASKERVILLES

Conrad peered back through the rapidly deepening twilight. He could see a bobbing line of torches, their flames leaping and twisting. The torches were held by mounted warriors, the light of the flames flashing on their helmets and armour. Ahead of the warriors bounded the dogs.

Conrad counted eleven torches. Therefore, at least eleven riders, and maybe some who did not carry torches. The rapidly advancing line was now little more than a kilometre behind him.

He swore mightily. It they had found the chopper, the dogs would already have his scent. This was no random hunt. The warriors were heading straight for him. The dogs were on his trail. Conrad began to run. If the worst came to the worst, he could always find some strategic point and start lasering. But that would be a very risky business. In daylight, no doubt, he could either laser them all or enough of them to discourage the rest. But darkness favoured the pursuers. He wouldn't be able to see the dogs until they were upon him, and by the time he had lasered a couple of riders, the rest would doubtless get the message and dump the torches.

As he ran, Conrad realized that darkness was not entirely on the side of the pursuers. The warriors would have to travel relatively slowly if their torches were to be of any practical use, and if they did not want to risk being thrown.

Conrad ran at a medium pace for ten minutes. Then he allowed himself a few precious seconds to get his breath and observe the progress of the pursuit. As far as he could judge, they still seemed to be about a kilometre behind him. If he wanted to increase the distance, he would have to go flat out. But he couldn't keep that up for long. He realized also that he could not even maintain his present pace for more than about half-an-hour.

It looked as if it were going to come to a shoot-out, after all. Rapidly, he dumped unnecessary equipment: the water canteen, the food packs, the med kit and the knife. He thought about calling the *Santa Maria* and asking Kwango to harness up and come and get him. But by the time Kwango's exo arrived, the show would be over. He couldn't even afford the time or the energy to make the call. Now only a miracle would get him out of the trap.

The baying of the dogs was louder. Conrad gripped his laser rifle tightly, turned and ran.

He got his miracle entirely by accident. He ran blindly into a stream and got thoroughly drenched. He dropped his laser rifle as the shock of the cold water hit him, and had to waste vital time groping on the stony bed until he found it. If the stream had been deep, he would have been in dead trouble.

He looked back and saw that the dogs and warriors were now only about half a kilometre behind him. His mind began to function once more. The stream! The stream would kill his scent.

He was already shivering, but he realized that it would be suicidal to get out of the water on the other side. The warriors would cross, and the dogs would pick up his scent once more. End.

Cautiously, he began to wade downstream. At times, the water barely covered his ankles; at times he was waist deep. Progress was slow, damnably slow. Looking back, he saw that he had only made about two hundred metres before the dogs and the first riders had reached the water's edge.

He stood still, patiently, and willed his teeth to stop chattering. If the riders came downstream, he would get out on the farther side and start burning when they tried to cross. In which case, too, he would hear the splashings of the dogs. And that would be a help. Maybe he could sweep-laser the bastards while they were still in the water.

It was only then that he remembered he had another advantage. He could switch to infra-red vision. Cursing himself for being such a fool, Conrad closed both his eye-lids and transferred the silver eyepatch to his bioeye. He waited for a few seconds, programming himself to accept the change in colour values.

Then he opened his infrared eye and gazed upstream. The torches were bright and blinding. But now he could "see" the heat radiation from the bodies of the warriors, their mounts, and their dogs.

The glowing dogs ran indecisively along the bank of the stream, barking their frustration. The warriors sat on their shaggy longhorns, waiting. One dog began to explore downstream. Conrad held his laser rifle ready. But then there was an excited barking from a dog that had ventured upstream. The rest followed its lead. Presently, the horsemen rode upstream to investigate.

Conrad offered up thanks for the stupid hound that had led them in the wrong direction. But he was still left with the persistent creature that was sniffing its way towards him. It was getting too close. The stream was not very wide. The dog, hot with running, glowed brightly, and an aureole of heat shimmered all round its head and body.

Conrad lifted his laser rifle slowly. He glanced upstream. The warriors were now more than a hundred metres away. But they might still hear this bloody dog if he didn't manage to kill it instantly.

The dog, sniffing and panting, was now no more than fifteen metres away. It was a massive beast. By infrared, it looked like a ghostly apparition. The hound of the Baskervilles!

Conrad centred on its skull and squeezed the trigger. He was instantly blinded as the fierce heat of the laser beam vapourized the dog's brain. The light was so bright that it caused physical pain. For a moment or two, he thought that his optic nerve must surely be destroyed.

But, presently, vision came back. The dog had died without a sound. It's still shimmering body lay inert on the far side of the stream.

He looked again at the torch-carrying warriors. They were now even further away. Once more Conrad blessed the hound that was following a false scent.

He felt deadly cold. His coverall was waterproof, but when he had fallen into the stream, enough water had penetrated the neck and arms and leg openings to make him wet all over.

"We'll soon cure this," he said to himself aloud.

He stood up and started to run. He ran for about ten minutes at top speed until he was thoroughly winded. Then his legs became rubber and he had to sit down.

He calculated that he must have covered at least three kilometres. Fortunately, the ground had been fairly level, and his infrared vision had helped him to avoid the occasional bushes and shrubs. His legs had failed him as he neared the top of a slight rise. As he sat recovering his breath, he turned and looked back.

In the distance, he could just make out the line of torches—dancing pinpoints of radiance. It looked as if the warriors were still on the other side of the stream. He hoped they would not discover the body of the hound he had burned. Because if they did, they would cross and pick up his scent once more.

Wearily, he picked himself up and started the march south once more. How many kilometres left to go? He didn't try to work it out. He didn't want to know. He was aware that he was cold and hungry and thirsty and that he now had nothing to eat or drink.

Again, he thought of calling the *Santa Maria* and asking Kwango to pick him up. But pride stopped him. That was what Lieutenant Smith had suggested—only to be flattened by her infallible commander. It would have given her one hell of a kick to know that Conrad realized he had made a bad decision.

He took the transceiver out of his pocket, merely to check that it was O.K. Water dripped from it. He pressed the transmit stud. Nothing happened. Dead as a dodo. He was glad he had made the decision not to call for Kwango before he knew the transceiver didn't work.

"Conrad," he said, "you are a stupid bastard. Atone for your sins. Get up and march."

He took a last look at the distant torches. They were nearer. The riders must have decided to cross the stream, anyway. Conrad got up and marched. Every now and then, he stopped and peered back through the darkness. There were no telltale glows now. Evidently he had shaken off the pursuit. He hoped so. The dogs would have been his undoing.

Time passed and, though he was tired, he managed to keep up a good pace. It was the only way to stay warm. The clothing under his coverall had dried out a little because of body warmth. But it was still damp enough, and the night air was cool enough to cancel the heat generated by his exertions.

After a couple of hours, he got a nasty shock. He discovered that he was being stalked. At first, he thought one of the dogs had picked up his trail. But then he dismissed the idea instantly. There was no sound, no barking or panting, no other animals around. no warriors following. Without his infrared eye, he would never have known he was being stalked, probably until it was too late.

The animal was about forty metres to the right. It's shimmering head-glow made the shape difficult to define. But it was much bigger than the hounds. As far as Conrad could make out, it was slightly taller, considerably longer and with a large head. It's stealthy movements suggested an abundance of grace and power—perhaps something like that of the Terran tiger.

He moved on a few paces, then stopped again. So did the animal. He repeated the performance—as did the animal. It had to be a carnivore.

Conrad raised his laser rifle, and at the same moment the beast decided to make its kill. With a great, snarling roar, it came at him. He had no time to take aim. The animal moved with fantastic speed and sprang. He managed to laser it in mid-air. But, though it was already dead or dying, the laser beam could not stop its momentum.

The growl died in the carnivore's throat, but its great body came hurtling on and knocked Conrad off his feet. A huge claw feebly raked his face before the beast was still.

Conrad picked himself up shakily. There was a stinging in his cheek, and something warm and wet trickled down to his chin. Gingerly, he felt the wounds. Three rather nasty slashes. Still, it could have been worse. Much worse.

His hand was wet and sticky. He wiped it on the grass and picked up his laser rifle.

"That's all I need!" he said bitterly. He could have used a large brandy and a med kit. But he didn't have a large brandy and a med kit. He took a deep breath, steadied himself, and began to march. And at each step, blood dripped from the end of his chin.

"Jesus Christ, what a trail I'm leaving!" he said with great anger. "If those bloody dogs get sensible, I've had it."

But luck was not entirely against him. Though he glanced back frequently with laser rifle always at the ready, there were no further signs of pursuit.

Phase Seven

KWANGO LOSES HIS COOL

Conrad made it back to the *Santa Maria* four hours after his original E.T.A. The blood still dripped from his face, he was deadly cold, and he was staggering like a drunken man.

As he approached the perimeter, a searchlight zeroed in on him. The light was blinding. Well, at last, a proper watch was being kept. More lights came on. The whole area surrounding the perimeter was illuminated.

Feebly, he tried to switch his silver eyepatch so that he would get normal vision. He couldn't manage it. His biohand was numb. He tried to transfer the laser rifle from his prosthetic hand to his biohand. He dropped it, bent down wearily and picked it up with the prosthetic hand.

Then there was a final surge of strength. "Kill some of those bloody lights!" he shouted. "It's me, Conrad. Send Matthew to bring me in." Then he fell flat on his face.

It wasn't Matthew who brought him in. It was Kwango. But Conrad didn't know.

When he returned to consciousness, he was in a bed in the sick bay. A drip-feed was putting plasma into him, Lieutenant Smith had a stethoscope pick-up on his chest, Kwango was gazing at him anxiously, and his face hurt like hell.

Feebly, he lifted a hand and tried to touch his cheek.

"Don't!" snapped Indira. "I have only just sewn your face together, and if you try to touch it, I'll break your arm."

Conrad tried to smile, and realized instantly that he had just made a dreadful mistake. The pain intensified. Beads of sweat formed on his forehead. He waited patiently until the throbbing had subsided.

Kwango gently wiped the sweat away. Indira slipped a needle into his arm.

"What the hell's that?" He remembered not to move his lips much. "If it's sleep juice, you'd better neutralize it fast."

"It is a mild analgesic, Commander," she said coldly. "You looked as if you needed it. But if, in my opinion, you need a knockout shot, you'll get one. And if there is any trouble from you, you'll get one anyway. It won't be the first time I have found it necessary to assume command."

Conrad, remembering the times he got himself into a mess on Kratos and Tantalus, wisely said nothing that would trigger the threat.

"Thank you, Lieutenant." He tried to make his voice sound humble, because there was no time for a knockout shot. "I'll try not to give any trouble. Actually, I feel pretty good, considering. Thanks for putting my face back together."

"My pleasure," said Indira. "Also, Commander, you feel pretty lousy and you know it. You are going to be left with three lovely scars. There may have to be skin grafts later—unless you don't mind looking like Son of Frankenstein. . . . Now, you have thirty minutes—after which time, if you don't go to sleep, you get the needle. Understood?"

"Understood, Lieutenant. Now what is the present state of play?"

It was Kwango who answered. "The bad news first, Boss?"

"Yes, but I was hoping that I was the only bad news. What is it?"

"We lost Dolfuss."

Conrad sat up, ignoring the pain that the effort cost him. "Dammit, you can't just lose Dolfuss. What happened?"

"She went out for a walk," said Kwango simply, "and we lost her."

Lieutenant Smith said, "She had been working hard in the lab all day. About an hour before sunset, she requested permission to go outside the perimeter defence for exercise. I gave permission and told her to stay within range of the screens and return before dark. She didn't stay within range, she didn't send any signals. When she didn't return before dark, Kurt got into his exo and went to look for her. He covered an area of three kilometres distance from the stockade, all the way round. No sign."

Black fury gripped Conrad. His face began to throb again. He tried to calm himself down. He failed.

"Lieutenant," he grated, "I hold you responsible. You can put your needles away. You are not fit to assume command."

"Commander," she retorted. "You are in a distressed condition—physically and mentally." She selected a hypo. "It is my professional opinion that you need to be tranquilized. Mr. Kwango, prepare the Commander's arm."

"One move, Kwango," said Conrad in a voice with a cutting edge, "and I'll dent your thick skull with my tin arm. After that, I'll log you for mutiny."

"Boss—" began Kwango.

Indira cut him short. "Unfit for command!" she stormed. "*I* didn't lose the chopper, get my face cut up and stagger back in an exhausted condition. You are out of your mind."

"Shut up, both of you!" For the first time since Conrad had known him, Kwango appeared to have lost his cool.

Conrad gazed at him, fascinated.

"Now listen good and hard, the pair of you. I don't care a shit whether you smash me, log me, or whatever. This is the third mission I've served with you, and it's the first time I don't like what I see. Last night, Commander, sir, it was your pleasure to remind everyone how much the meal cost that only you and me ate while it was hot. I now remind you both that today you have made mistakes that cost a hell of a lot more than that meal. I fancy you, Lieutenant, as you know. I lifted you out of the trap, Commander, on Tantalus, as you may recall. But I am not going to see this mission put at risk because you both want to play sexual games. If you crash out now, I'll kill you both and abort the mission. At least some of us will get back to Terra. End of message." Kwango was shaking. He was shaking with anger.

Conrad was the first to speak. "Kurt, I regret to say this, but you are absolutely right. Thank you for reminding me that I have been a bloody fool." He turned to Indira. "Lieutenant Smith, I apologise for stupid remarks uttered in anger. I hope you will forgive me. I have no excuse, and I think——"

"James," she cut in, "both Kurt and I know to our cost that you can be hell to live with. But we also know other things, which I will not mention because your ego is quite big enough." She glanced at the hypo she was holding, smiled faintly, and put it down. "It is my professional opinion that we all need large whiskies."

"Praise de Lord!" said Kwango. He gave an order over the intercom. Presently, the robot Mark appeared with a bottle and three glasses.

"Who is on the screens?" asked Conrad.

"Matthew," said Indira. "Ustinov got square eyes. I gave her a sedative."

Kwango poured the drinks. Big ones.

"Now, Boss, we'll all get sensible. And for starters, you can make with the funnies. We know how you lost the chopper, but how come you stagger back, falling about, with those handsome features somewhat carved?"

Succinctly, Conrad told him.

Kwango whistled. "These people are very persistent

That will teach the bitch, he thought. That will teach her that personalities don't count in this game. Results are all that matter. And it doesn't matter how you get the results—just so long as you get them.

He lifted high and swung north.

Presently, he radioed the *Santa Maria*. "Chopper calling. All well, Ustinov?"

"All well, Commander. I checked with Kurt. He said to tell you he was making good progress."

"Fine." Conrad laughed, remembering the woebegone expression on Kwango's face when the young Zelosian had a go at him. "Tell Kurt it will be adequate if he speaks the language with some fluency before the day is out. I'm heading north. I want to take a quick look at the city. Over and out."

Conrad held to an altitude of one thousand metres and brought his airspeed up to 300 k.p.h. He was eager to take a good look at Enigma. The pix Lieutenant Smith had brought back were of good quality, but they could not convey the feel of the place. He wondered how low he could risk going in. That, of course, raised another problem—don't irritate the natives more than you have to. They had already been subjected to one aerial scrutiny, which must have angered them somewhat because of their inability to strike back. And they had taken a beating yesterday on the ground.

The diplomatic thing to do would be to keep—as they used to say—a low profile for a while. But the exigencies of the mission would not allow for that. Zelos had to be proved. One way or the other.

Conrad shrugged. In for a penny, in for a pound. Idly, he wondered how that phrase had originated. What it really meant was—go for broke.

The Zelosians, a warlike people, were unlikely to regard these intruders into their world as harbingers of good will—particularly after yesterday's shoot-out. So, really, the harm had already been done, and it wouldn't much affect the issue whether he went in as low as possible, or surveyed the city from a discreet altitude.

He glanced at the land below. It was getting more hilly and less wooded now. Here and there, small herds hombres—as I already know to my cost. Have another whiskey, Boss."

Conrad forgot himself and briefly tried to smile. "That tells me you have more bad news."

"There is a little good news," said Kwango. "There is more bad than good. I'll make it a sandwich. The good bit in the middle. One: the cyphers on that skin Lieutenant Smith brought back have been decoded. Message reads, 'You, who slew our brothers, know that vengeance will be taken. You, who dwell in the iron tower, know that Scolopen marches against you. You, whose days are short, make peace with your gods . . .' And how do you like that, Boss?"

"I don't. Who the hell is Scolopen?"

Kwango poured more whiskey. "Have the good news first. I got a working Zelosian vocabulary—about eight hundred words. Me and the computer, that is." He scratched his head. "That 'boy' was very high-spirited, Commander. I had to persuade him somewhat before he made all the noises I needed."

"He is still alive, I trust?" Conrad inquired drily.

"Yes, Boss, but he is not too happy."

"No permanent damage?"

"I don't think so."

Indira said, "When Kurt had finished with him, I shot him full of tranquilizer and checked him over. Bad bruising, but he'll live."

"Thanks for getting the vocabulary, Kurt. Can you use it?"

"Most of it, Boss. Hell, I've had less than a day to master the syntax."

"Can you speak Zelosian if you have to?"

"With luck and a fair wind."

"O.K. That's not bad. Now give me the nasty bit that you have been saving up until you filled me full of whisky."

Kwango took a deep breath. "We scored three lemons, Boss. This kid is Orylos, son of Scolopen, Emperor of the Known World. He is the best beloved of the big boy on this planet. And how is that for bad luck?"

Conrad sipped his whiskey. "So the shit hits the fan . . .

Indira, I want something that is going to keep me alert for the next twenty-four Z-hours. Can you do it?"

"James, you are driving yourself too hard."

"Can you do it?"

She sighed, then selected a hypo and a phial. "I can do it."

He caught her glance. "O.K. We compromise. I'll rest for a couple of hours or so. Then give me the zip juice. . . . Kurt, how good are you at brainwashing?"

Kwango grinned. "Not bad, Boss—judging by the last half hour."

Conrad knew better than to smile. "That's the old, modest Kwango that we have learned to love. As soon as it's daybreak, make sure this Orylos character has a good meal. Then give him the soft sell. Tell him we like him very much and that we like his father very much and that we want to be friends with all Zelosians, and all the rest of it. Give him some presents—if we have any items of equipment he can't hurt himself with—and tell him he's been ill. Tell him he's nearly recovered now, and we are going to send him back to his father."

Kwango shrugged. "This boy isn't stupid, Boss. I had to use him to decode the message. That gave him a big kick. He said he didn't care a Zelosian damn what we did to him. He said that when Daddy gets cross, he really gets cross, and when he really gets cross, he is a very hard man. He is of the opinion that Daddy is going to stamp us into the ground while he thinks of something *really* nasty to do."

"With what?" asked Conrad. "Daddy doesn't know about lasers and exos and minefields."

"I know that, Boss," said Kwango patiently. "But I learned a few things talking to the boy. These people are fighting folk. They value strength and courage above everything else. They also have some very strange notions about honour. When it comes to honour, they don't count the cost. They don't want to know. This Orylos, he thinks that Scolopen will march at the head of his Immortals. And that don't sound too good."

"What the devil are the Immortals?"

"The best fighting men on Zelos, Boss. The élite cadre

of Scolopen's army. One thousand strong. Every man has killed three men in duels or in the Games. I'll tell you about the duelling system and the Games—what I understand of it—later. But the situation looks a trifle bleak."

Conrad was tired and in pain. He wasn't thinking too clearly. "Are you telling me we can't handle one thousand tough savages? Why, two men in exos could—"

"Boss, you miss the point. If we can't get friendly with these characters, we are going to have to take them all out. And I mean *all*. I get the impression that while they can still stand, they fight. And how would you like to have to explain to the eggheads back at U.N. on Terra that you had to wipe the élite of Zelos before the natives got docile enough to accept colonization?"

"Christ!" said Conrad. "One court-martial is enough. Do what you can, Kurt. Promise him the Earth, tell him we're all God's children. Do what you can."

Phase Eight

CLEAR THE DECKS FOR ACTION

Conrad managed to get nearly four hours of rest. He had been very careful to settle down on the undamaged side of his face. Presently, the pain faded and exhaustion, plus whisky, triumphed. He slept well.

He had asked to be wakened at daybreak, but, by the time he had drifted off, daybreak was little more than an hour away. Lieutenant Smith let him sleep on. Wisely, he did not complain.

When he came down to the saloon for breakfast, he felt in reasonably good condition—apart from the stiffness in his cheek. Lieutenant Smith had prescribed liquid food only—to his intense distaste. He countermanded the order and asked Mark, the robot on saloon duty, for bacon and eggs. Chewing the bacon hurt like hell, but he managed to get two eggs, some bread and two cups of coffee down. He felt better.

The only other Expendable taking a late breakfast was Kwango. He looked haggard. Conrad guessed that he had not slept at all.

"Where are the rest, Kurt?"

Kwango briefed him. "Lieutenant Smith is on the nav deck; Ustinov is trying to chat up our young friend—on the right side of the pen; Mencken and Gautier are out in the hovercar, quartering to the north, looking for Dolfuss; and all is well with the world."

"I take it you have already had a fireside chat with Orylos. How did it work out?"

Kwango shrugged. "Not too well, Boss. He don't take kindly to brainwashing. . . . These people have a very peculiar psychology. If they can't eat it, screw it, or conquer it, they just don't want to know. I had to hit him somewhat before he would even listen to me. He's a very obstinate young man."

"You didn't break anything?" asked Conrad anxiously. "We are going to need him in one piece, I think."

"Not even his spirit," said Kwango. He sighed. "The boy is convinced that Scolopen is going to take us out in a very interesting fashion. His only reason for staying alive, he says, is so that he can see us chopped. After that, he proposes to chop himself, to expiate the terrible sin/shame/crime of being taken prisoner."

"That doesn't sound too good, Kurt. Did you try the big brother approach?"

"He doesn't want to know about big brothers. But I picked up a lot of useful background. You want it now?"

Conrad finished his coffee. "Yes, Kurt, I want it now. Something tells me we are running out of time."

Rapidly and efficiently, Kwango gave all the information he had gleaned. The real name of the city that Conrad had designated as Enigma was Rossvallin. It was, in effect, a city-state. Scolopen, King of Rossvallin and Emperor of the Known World, Triple Winner of the Games, had absolute authority. But he was not an hereditary king. Each year, he had to defend his title against the Winner of the Games.

As Kwango understood it, war had long ago been abolished on Zelos. Rossvallin, the largest city-state, dominated all the others. Altogether, there were ten—most of them being no more than large villages by Terran standards. Each year at the close of the Games, the ten chieftains renewed their allegiance to the King of Rossvallin.

So far as Kwango could ascertain, the total population of the planet was no more than about thirty or forty thousand, all centred on a few thousand square kilometres near the northern coast of the great continent. From time to time, successive kings had dispatched expeditions inland, but they had not discovered any other people. Despite their similarity to the ancient Vikings of Earth, the Zelosians were no great seafarers. Their exploration of the oceans had been very limited—partly because they believed their world was flat and if one sailed far enough he would very likely fall off it.

War had been abolished when the kingdom of Rossvallin became strong enough to dominate the rest. Long ago, the Zelosians had rightly perceived that war was an untidy and unpredictable way of settling disputes. It could bring about the destruction of an entire community and, in any case, those whose cause was just did not necessarily triumph.

But because the Zelosians were a tough, aggressive people—and wished to remain that way—two vital war substitutes had evolved. One was the Duel and the other was the War Games.

Under Zelosian law, no man had the right to beget a child unless he had defeated or killed an opponent in a public duel, brought about by a legitimate grievance. The legitimacy of the grievance was determined by the Judges of the Duel—who were, in effect, the Zelosian equivalent of lawyers. Every man had a right to refuse a duel, though he would suffer the consequence of social disgrace. If a man wished to beget another child, he would have to gain victory in another duel, and so on. If two or more men desired the same woman, the matter would be settled by a duel or duels, the woman's preference being deemed irrelevant.

"It looks as if women don't have much status in this society," commented Conrad.

"Boss, they don't have any status. They aren't even second-class citizens. They are just pleasure machines, breeding machines and cheap labour. If they speak before they are spoken to, they get knocked on the head. If they won't open their legs when required, they get knocked on the head. And if they don't produce a male child when they get fertilized, they still get knocked on the head. . . . Most self-respecting Zelosians have at least two or three wives, mistresses or slaves. The women do all the hard work. The men just beat their chests and try to kill each other when they get bored."

"Interesting," mused Conrad. "We might be able to make use of that. Now tell me about the Games."

The War Games of Zelos have something in common with the Olympic Games of Earth. There is one vital difference. No one got killed in the Olympic Games—except by accident—but in the War Games, the carnage is heavy. There are two classes of events: one non-mortal, the other mortal. The non-mortal events include running, jumping, swimming, riding, wrestling. The winning of any of these events brings a certain amount of respect, but little else. The mortal events are all variations on the theme of gladiatorial combat. There are some team events, but the great emphasis is on single combat with axe, sword, dagger and other weapons, except the bow.

"So you see, Boss," concluded Kwango, "this culture is really a paradox. Intertribal war doesn't exist, but the Games represent a kind of stylized warfare. These people are death-oriented. They got a kind of Valhalla, too, where all warriors who die bravely are supposed to go and get it off with bouncy ladies when they get bored with fighting and drinking."

"You managed to get a great deal of data out of that young man," commented Conrad.

Kwango winced as he touched various tender parts of his anatomy. "It wasn't easy, Boss, as you saw. That joker has some interesting tricks. But I had a bit of luck. Remember when he first spoke, and I repeated it? That was the bit of luck. It is the ritual greeting between warriors who know they are of equal calibre, or something like that. I got a good working knowledge of the language, but I'm still having difficulty with the nuances and idiom. The trouble is—"

Lieutenant Smith called over the intercom from the nav deck.

"Hal and Jean-Pierre have found Hildegarde."

"Good. She's alive?"

"Alive but not happy, I think."

"Are they bringing her in?"

"That's the problem, Commander. She appears to be naked, or almost naked, and tied to a wooden frame on a cart drawn by a couple of longhorns. She is near the head of a column of heavily armed and mounted warriors coming this way. Hal and Jean-Pierre haven't gone in close. They have laser rifles in the hovercar, of course. They have grounded the car in a hollow, about three kilometres ahead of the column. They don't think they were seen. Hal spotted the column with his binoculars when it was about six or seven kilometres away."

"What is the strength of these bastards?"

"About a thousand, Hal thinks."

Kwango whistled. "The kid was right. Scolopen is sending in his Immortals."

"How far away are they and what is their rate of progress?"

"About twenty-five kilometres and they don't seem to be in a hurry. Estimated speed about eight or nine k.p.h. . . . Jean-Pierre wants to wait until the column is close to the hovercar, then go in on high lift with lasers burning at maximum. He thinks there is a good chance he can cause the longhorns to stampede and then burn enough of their riders to buy the time to get Hildegarde. Hal doesn't like the odds. The trouble is that one of them would have to be out of the hovercar probably for a minute or more to collect Hildegarde."

"Hal is dead right," snapped Conrad. "Dolfuss got herself into this mess. We can't risk two men and the hovercar to get her out. Their bowmen are good. Dolfuss hasn't got her armorlite jacket and she, at least, would be a pin cushion. Hook me in direct."

"Will do."

"This is Conrad. Do you read me?"

"I read you, Commander." It was Mencken's voice.

"Good. Now hear this. Take no offensive action. Repeat, take no offensive action. Do you read?"

"I read."

"Track the column until it is within ten kilometres of base and you are sure it is heading for us. Then get back here fast. Try to keep out of sight. Over and out."

Jean-Pierre cut in. "Commander, we can't just leave Hildegarde like that. She is an Earth woman. Those pigs have her stretched out like an animal ready for slaughter. God knows what they have already—"

"She's an Expendable," said Conrad harshly, "as we all are. She disobeyed orders and this is the result. You make one move to get her now and you'll be signing her death warrant. Besides, things are bad enough already. I'm damned if I'm going to precipitate an almost certain bloodbath because one Expendable went over the hill. Do you read me?"

"I read you, Commander, but I no longer respect you."

"Obey me, that's all."

"You're running the show, Commander." It was Mencken's voice. Don't fret about Jean-Pierre. He's all steamed up with Gallic temperament, but he knows how to obey orders."

"Thanks, Hal. See you soon. Over and out." Conrad turned to Kwango. "It looks as if we are going to need your linguistic skills pretty soon, Kurt. Scolopen and his friendly neighbourhood Immortals seem to be in the mood for a shoot-out. You are going to have to talk them down."

Kwango sighed. "I'll do my best, Boss. But we are dealing with a very proud people. Like you, dey got de kamikaze syndrome."

"*I* do not have the kamikaze syndrome, Kwango," said Conrad fiercely. "All I am concerned with is proving this planet."

Kwango gave a faint smile. "O.K., Commander. That's your story. . . . I hope they ain't messed up Hildegarde too much. I fancy that bird."

Conrad swallowed the last of his coffee. The effort hurt. "Now, I suppose, we have to clear the decks for action. We have, at best, about three hours."

Phase Nine

ACTION STATIONS

It was a fine, warm morning—for which Conrad was profoundly grateful. There were fleecy clouds in the sky, but a weather report from Ustinov indicated that rain was not likely to fall before evening, which suited Conrad well. He did not want his dealings with Scolopen to be influenced by the state of the weather.

Two Z-hours had passed since Mencken had reported back. There was no sign yet of the hovercar or of Scolopen's advancing column. Maybe the Zelosians had stopped for a break.

Conrad scratched his silver eyepatch, then fingered his damaged face cautiously. Lieutenant Smith had sprayed syntheskin over her needlework. The cheek was a bit twitchy, but it felt smooth and half numb. It would be impossible for anyone more than five metres away from him to know that Conrad had been injured.

He was standing with Kwango on one of the raised platforms that the robots had hastily constructed at strategic points along the inside of the stockade. The platform was by the side of the gate. Since the gate faced north and the Zelosians were coming from the north, Conrad thought this the most likely place for confrontation. Nevertheless, he had allowed for the possibility of the Zelosians trying to box clever. He could switch defence and fire power to any point within seconds.

Close by his feet lay Jean-Pierre Gautier's masterpiece —the command console for all the radio mines round the perimeter. It was a complex black box with a three-deep circle of tiny studs on its control panel. Press one, and a mine could be detonated by itself. Sweep a finger round the outside circle, and all the third ring mines would blow. Similarly, with the second and inner circles. Whatever else happened, Scolopen could not take the *Santa Maria*. Briefly, Conrad felt sorry for him. There was the Emperor of the Known World, at the head of his élite corps, coming to take out the people who had invaded his territory. And he didn't stand a chance.

The entire base was now ready to receive him—peacefully or otherwise. Conrad devoutly hoped it would not be otherwise. Because the Zelosians had this thing about courage and combat and physical prowess, they would probably get quite a lot of themselves killed before they got discouraged. But Conrad had a few tricks up his sleeve. He did not want to demoralize them—that, as Kwango had pointed out, would probably destroy their entire culture pattern—and he only wanted to deter them. The ideal situation would be a standoff which left them their pride. Most important of all, Scolopen must not be humiliated before his people.

Ustinov reported from the nav deck. "The hovercar is coming in, Commander. Matthew estimates range at eight kilometres and speed 40 k.p.h. We can now just see the head of the column through the observation panel."

Conrad peered anxiously ahead but could see nothing—which was to be expected. The nav deck was eighty metres up, commanding a good view of the terrain.

"Good. Get down here and join us. Matthew can take over. . . . Do you read me, Matthew?"

Matthew's imperturbable metallic voice came over the transceiver. "I read you clearly, Commander."

"You will keep me informed of the progress of the column. I wish to know the number of mounted men, the number of men travelling on foot, what equipment they have and what arms they carry. And, at the earliest possible moment, I wish to have information on the condition of Hildegarde Dolfuss."

"Decisions noted, Commander. Execution proceeds. I am now using the manual telescope at magnification 30. Report on the condition of Miss Dolfuss is as follows: she is alive and apparently not seriously injured. She is strapped or bound to a rectangular wooden frame, estimated dimensions approximately one metre by two metres. Most of her clothing has been removed and she is completely naked from the waist down. The frame is fixed vertically on a four-wheeled cart, drawn by two animals designated as longhorns. There are discolourations on her face and the exposed parts of her body. Such discolourations are consonant with those known to appear on human flesh after it has been subjected to sharp impact. Estimated number of visible discolourations is—"

"Cancel!" snapped Conrad irritably. "You have taken a bloody long time to tell us that she has been given a going-over."

"Query term: Going-over, sir?"

"Cancel term. Report on the column."

"Decision noted. Execution proceeds. Strength of column is as follows: excluding Miss Dolfuss, one thousand and one armed and mounted men riding in lines of four, with one mounted man leading. All arms are not visible, but sample analysis yields the following probabilities: each man has two or more weapons. Weapons visible include swords, axes, bows and arrows, lances. The men wear helmets and some body armour. Some men have armour on their right arm only. At the rear of the column there are several vehicles drawn by longhorns. These vehicles appear to support machines, as yet unidentifiable. Preliminary report terminates."

"Siege engines!" exploded Conrad. "They are bringing up bloody siege engines." Suddenly, he realized that if Scolopen's Immortals started hurling sizeable missiles, the *Santa Maria* was at risk. It was now more important than ever that the confrontation didn't result in a shoot-out.

Hastily, Conrad reviewed his preparations. At present, the minefield was inactive and under radio control, but a master switch would make all the mines respond to pressure, instead of radio detonation. Lieutenant Smith was already harnessed into an exo and lying concealed behind the stockade. Ustinov, now armed with a laser rifle and wearing an armorlite jacket, was on a platform on the other side of the gate. The robots, Peter and Paul, were standing by in the engine room and air-lock respectively, in case the situation got bad enough for an emergency lift. Mark, Luke and John, also laser-armed, were on platforms on the south side of the stockade, with instructions to remain concealed and to take no offensive action unless the stockade was in danger of being breached. When Mencken and Gautier returned, decided Conrad, Mencken—who had considerable talent with an exo—could harness up, while Gautier joined Ustinov.

"Boss," said Kwango. "I don't like the idea of siege engines too much. Why not let me take an exo and go out and stampede those longhorns? It will save a lot of trouble."

"Wrong, Kurt. It will only delay a lot of trouble and maybe increase it. Also, the moment you get tough, Hildegarde will collect a bellyfull of arrows. Also, I want you here to talk for me. Somehow, we have to negotiate."

The hovercar was not visible from the platform. Conrad used his transceiver. "Peter, Paul, open the gate. When the hovercar has entered the defence perimeter, close the gates again and return to position."

"Decision noted, Commander. Execution proceeds."

Matthew reported from the nav deck. "Commander, the helicopter is now visible. It is on a vehicle at the rear of the column. Revised estimate of arms is—"

"Terminate report," snapped Conrad. "I get the picture."

"Query, sir: What picture? I have not relayed any visual—"

"Cancel statement."

"Decision noted. Execution proceeds."

The hovercar came through the gateway. Mencken grounded it and got out, followed by Gautier. They spotted Conrad and came up to the platform.

"Hal, get into an exo and lie low. Jean-Pierre, take your laser and join Jane on the other side of the gate. No burning unless I say so. Understood?"

"Understood, Commander." Gautier sounded sullen, probably because he had been deprived of doing his Galahad act.

The column was now clearly visible from the platform.

Conrad called Matthew. "How long before the bastards hit us?"

"Query term 'bastards', sir," responded Matthew.

Conrad passed a hand wearily over his forehead. His face hurt, he wasn't feeling too good and he was fed up with robot-ese. Sometimes, he wondered if Matthew had developed a sadistic sense of humour.

"Cancel statement. Supply E.T.A. of column of armed men."

"Decision noted. Execution proceeds. E.T.A. of armed column is thirty-eight minutes from now, plus or minus five percent. It is possible that column may halt, in which case E.T.A. will be revised upon resumption of progress and observation of rate of—"

"Terminate report." Conrad turned to Kwango. "We have to sell refrigerators to a bunch of Eskimos."

"I know that, Boss."

"Think we can do it?"

Kwango shrugged. "The age of miracles may not yet be past."

"They have the chopper and they have Dolfuss. I think they want to rub our noses in something unpleasant."

"Cheer up, Boss. We got Orylos."

"Yes. I wonder if that aggressive bastard Scolopen cares very much whether his son lives or dies."

Stage Three

THE WAR GAMES

Phase One

DEATH OF AN IMMORTAL—
QUEEN WITH A BARE BOTTOM

The man leading the column was, presumably, Scolopen, Emperor of the Known World, King of Rossvallin, Triple Winner of the Games. Conrad studied him through binoculars. He was a magnificent specimen. He wore a winged helmet, golden in colour, that flashed in the sunlight. He carried a small shield on one arm. His chest was bare; but his sword arm was sheathed in golden chain mail, as were his legs. A great sword hung in a scabbard from his waist. His hair was long, yellow, curly. His eyes were blue. Viking blue. His face was that of a proud, hard man. Once again, Conrad marvelled at the fantastic similarity of these people and the ancient sea bandits of Earth.

Scolopen halted his column almost a hundred metres from the stockade. Immediately behind him were five ranks, each of four mounted warriors, all of them looking very formidable. Behind them was the cart on which Hildegarde Dolfuss lay, lashed to the wooden frame. Conrad inspected her closely. Her belly and legs were badly bruised, as was her face. One of the eyes was puffy and closed. But she breathed and she was conscious.

Scolopen signalled casually with his hand. The column fanned out and drew up line abreast, three deep, with regular gaps in the ranks. The precision and speed of the operation drew Conrad's reluctant admiration. This was a highly disciplined body of men. The longhorns they rode seemed to respond to the rider's will instinctively.

"Boss," said Kwango nervously, "I don't like this

situation too much. We can't burn all those characters if they decide to charge."

"No," said Conrad, "but if it is a question of survival we can blow them. . . . If they decide to charge—which I don't think they are going to do—we'll switch the mines to pressure. Then it's goodbye Immortals and hello court-martial. . . . Get your loud-hailer, black man. You are about to speak soothing words of peace."

Through the gaps in the ranks of the Immortals, various wooden vehicles were trundled. They were indeed siege engines: ballistae, catapults, mobile battering rams. They were ready for business.

Scolopen urged his mount a few metres forward.

Two mounted men came out of the ranks and stationed themselves on each side of the king. They raised what looked like silver hunting horns to their lips and blew a long, melodious blast. Then, simultaneously, they uttered a few words.

"What are they saying?" asked Conrad.

Kwango scratched his head. "Rough translation only, Boss. Silence, doomed ones. Scolopen speaks."

"Make back: We are not doomed, but we listen."

Kwango used the loud-hailer. Many of the Zelosians looked surprised. Some laughed. Maybe, thought Conrad, they were surprised at Kwango's use of their language. Maybe they were laughing at the notion that Conrad and his people did not think they were doomed.

Scolopen came a little closer. So did his heralds.

The king gazed hard at the stockade and fingered the hilt of his sword. Then he spoke. He spoke slowly in a strong voice—doubtless realizing that the strangers were not very familiar with his language—and the words came over loud and clear.

"Give me the sense of it, Kurt."

"He greets the uninvited strangers who have brought death as their gift. He says he has come to return the gift. He says he will give us a little time to make peace with our gods before he sends us to them for judgement."

"Tell him that we would rather use the time for talking."

Kwango used the loud-hailer once more. There was a brief silence, then Scolopen replied.

Kwango translated. "He says that wise men would choose to pray. Only fools would waste their breath. Nevertheless, he will listen for a short space. He asks if I of the black face am the chief of this curious tribe."

"Put this as well as you can: Tell him that I, Conrad, of the Silver Patch, Lord of the Sky, Master of Fire, Commander of Giants, am the chief of this tribe. Tell him I wish for peace and friendship, but that I can strike dreadfully if provoked. And tell him you are my mouthpiece."

"Hell, Boss, I don't have the words for all that crap."

"Do the best you can. Just make me sound bloody powerful."

Kwango rolled his eyes and started to speak once more in halting Zelosian. When he had finished speaking, Scolopen laughed. So did his Immortals. The king held up his hand for silence.

He spoke slowly so that his words would be understood. "Know this, Conrad of the Silver Patch—friendship between your people and mine is not possible. Blood has been shed, vengeance must be taken. My son no longer sits at his father's table, and other good men have died as well. For this alone a high price must be paid. I have one of your women, as you perceive. She has provided some amusement for my captains but she experienced little joy in such matters. Presently, you may watch her die. Also, I have the machine that winged noisily through the sky. Now, its wings are silent. You speak brave words, Commander of Giants. But I see no giants and I see no army. Your time has come."

Kwango translated rapidly.

Conrad said, "Tell him his son is alive and well. Tell him that we will exchange Orylos for Hildegarde. Say to him that in our country brave men do not butcher women. Tell him we still want peace."

"O.K. Boss. But this Zelosian talk is giving me one hell of a headache."

"Live with it, Kwango. By the look of it, Dolfuss has worse aches in worse places."

While Kwango was speaking, Hildegarde struggled weakly with her bonds and seemed to be trying to say or shout something. Conrad tried hard to hear, but Kurt's amplified voice drowned her words. The effort seemed to have exhausted her. She slumped. Her head sank forward, and it looked as if she had passed out. Conrad hoped so. The next few minutes were going to decide a lot of things —not the least, whether Hildegarde lived or died.

Scolopen's reply was disdainful.

Kwango translated. "He says you lie. He says his son died in battle. He says that you are no longer Lord of the Sky because he has your sky machine. And he does not believe you are Master of Fire and Commander of Giants, because he hasn't seen any fire and he hasn't seen any giants. He says he hopes we will die like men and that our blood will not dishonour the swords of his warriors. And he says get ready for the showdown."

"This character is setting himself up for a dose of cultural shock," said Conrad grimly. "Tell him this. One, his son will presently walk through the gateway to join him. Two, I will demonstrate that I am Master of Fire. Three, he will see my giants."

While Kwango was using the loud-hailer, Conrad spoke into his transceiver. "Matthew, detail two robots to get the Zelosian out of his pen and through the gateway. He is not to be damaged. Do you read me?"

"I read you, Commander. Decision noted. Execution proceeds."

"Lieutenant Smith, Mencken, as of now you are giants. Stand up and be recognized when I say go."

Kwango had finished speaking. Scolopen replied briefly.

"What does he say?"

"Not to put too fine a point upon it, Boss, he says you are full of crap."

Conrad glanced down into the compound. The robots were already carrying the weakly struggling Orylos toward the gates. Conrad smiled grimly. The Zelosian's eyes were wide with fear. He had seen the robots operating before, and Kwango had explained to him that they were mechanical slaves, but this was his first close contact, and he was obviously half out of his mind.

"Make back to Scolopen: I am a man of my word. I

109

return to him his son, who is a great warrior. Say also that I should be proud to have such a son."

The gates were opened, Orylos was released and thrust outside. As soon as the robots had let him go, he recovered his wits. He gazed for a moment or two at the ranks of the Immortals, then walked towards Scolopen. The gates were closed, and the robots returned to their defence positions.

There was an exchange of words between Orylos and his father.

Scolopen spoke once more. "I thank you for the return of my son, Conrad. I thank you for your high opinion of him. He has asked me to spare the life of the black man with the hard head who, he says, is also a warrior of great heart. This request, I grant. Further, before you are destroyed, I grant you the right to dispatch the woman of your own tribe who is dishonoured."

Kwango translated. Conrad said: "Make back: In our eyes, the woman is not dishonoured, Scolopen. Only those who have laid violent hands upon her are dishonoured. You are a great king and one whom I think has much wisdom. Return her to us."

There was much shouting and raising of weapons in the ranks of the Immortals when Kwango gave Conrad's reply. Presently Scolopen held up his hand, and the tumult ceased.

"You have insulted seven of my captains, Conrad of the Silver Patch. In our country such an insult is cause for a fight to the death. You cannot meet seven such as these. But you can either die at the hands of one of them, or at my hands, for though you gave back my son, you cannot give back the dead. Which, then, is it to be?"

When Kwango had given Conrad the translation, he said, "I can't keep this up much longer, Boss. My brain is turning to porridge."

"Your brain, Kwango, like the rest of you, is expendable," snapped Conrad. "Make back: I do not wish to meet you or any of your warriors in battle, Scolopen. Enough blood has been shed. Let there be peace between us."

Again there was much noise in the Zelosian ranks. It

was louder than before. An arrow whanged into the stockade just below Conrad.

Scolopen glanced behind him and loudly uttered one word. The noise stopped. Slowly, one man held up his bow. Scolopen pointed at the man. Instantly, the warrior nearest to him drew a sword and expertly sliced off the bowman's head. The body toppled from the saddle.

"Conrad, the time for words is over. My men are impatient, as you see. They call you a liar and a coward. You will not face any of the captains you have insulted, and they say you are not a Master of Fire or a Commander of Giants, since they have seen neither."

When Conrad had heard the translation, he said: "Tell him again I am a man of my word. Tell him again that I still wish for peace, but he is about to witness my power. Say that if any of his seven captains still have the courage after they see what is about to happen, I will face the best of them alone. Got that?"

"Boss, this interpreter kick is killing me."

"So I'll buy flowers and mourn at your grave. Get the message across."

While Kwango was speaking, Conrad radioed Mencken who, concealed behind the stockade, still lay harnessed in his exoskeleton. "O.K., Hal, stand up and join the party."

"Shall I come up, too?" asked Lieutenant Smith.

"Not yet, Lieutenant. Let's give it to them a bit at a time." Conrad took up his laser rifle. Meanwhile, the vast eight metre shape of the exoskeleton rose, towering over the stockade.

There were cries of awe from the ranks of the Zelosians. But Scolopen either was not impressed or concealed his reaction expertly.

"Conrad of the Silver Patch, I acknowledge that you have shown us a giant, strange of shape and appearance and doubtless cunningly fashioned by your craftsmen. But, as we destroyed your machine of the sky, we will also destroy your machine of the ground." He gestured behind him at the ballistae. "We, also, have formidable machines."

"Cunning bastard!" exclaimed Conrad when Kwango

had finished translating. "He is trying to put heart back into his men." He used the transceiver. "Hal, how good are you at catching?"

"Could have made pro baseball ten years ago if I'd wanted."

"Good. Make ready to catch a fifty to one hundred kilo baseball and toss it back exactly where it came from on the word of command."

The metal arms of the exoskeleton moved in grotesque mimicry of a man flexing his muscles—which was exactly what Hal Mencken was doing.

"No sweat, Commander. You have the right man for the job."

Conrad turned to Kwango. "Tell Scolopen to take out my giant with one of his rock-throwers. Tell him the giant will not move. And wish him good luck."

"I hope you know what you are doing, Boss."

"I know what I'm doing. Make the signal."

It took two men to lift the stone ball into the launching cup of the ballista. Conrad looked at the brawny men who were loading the machine and made rapid calculations.

He talked to Mencken. "It's about one hundred and twenty-five kilos, Hal. Can you handle it?"

"I can handle it." Mencken moved the thick vanadium steel fingers of both exohands. "Not to worry, Commander. Those boys are going to be sorry they joined this ball game."

The missile was perfectly aimed. It hurtled straight towards the control crown of the exo. And Mencken caught it perfectly, using one exohand only. He tossed the great rounded rock into the air. Fifty metres up it went. Then he caught it with the other hand.

"How'm I doing, Commander?"

"You have just earned an extra booze ration."

Scolopen observed the feat in blank astonishment. His Immortals made sounds that were pleasing to Conrad's ears.

"Return it," said Conrad. "Take out the ballista that threw it."

Mencken's aim was good. The ballista was shattered.

Several longhorns nearby reared and threw their riders.

"Now we get the show on the road," said Conrad. He used his transceiver. "Stand up, Lieutenant Smith, and be counted. Let them see we have more than one giant."

Then Conrad lasered a hundred-metre sweep of the tall, green grass, exactly halfway between Scolopen and the stockade. When the flames had died down, he detonated six units of the external ring of Gautier's mines for good measure. The noises were satisfyingly loud, the craters were impressively deep.

When the smoke had died down, he saw that Scolopen and his Immortals had backed away. Gratifyingly, a number of riderless longhorns were now careering away from the base. Almost a quarter of the Immortals were now on foot. Scolopen remained mounted.

"Now tell him this, Kurt. I keep my word, but I also wish for peace between us. Say also that there is one matter to settle. Let the best of his dishonoured captains step forward unarmed. Say I will come out to meet him—unarmed."

"Boss, you are in no condition for fancy games. Your face is messed up, you ain't had much sleep, and if some tough Zelosian—and they come tough—ruins de Lieutenant's fancy needlework, she is going to get cross."

"Make the message. You worry too much."

Kwango used the loud-hailer. Scolopen gently urged his longhorn forward, until he was within twenty metres of the stockade.

He spoke to Kwango, but his eyes were on Conrad.

"Your machines make you powerful, Conrad of the Silver Patch. You spoke the truth. It is strange for a man with such power at his command to speak of peace. Also it is strange that you should risk defeat in combat for a woman. Is it a fight to the death?"

"Make back," said Conrad when he had the translation. "In our country, women are people, not animals to be used. Say that I agree to a fight to the death, and that I will strike once only. Say that we will again talk of peace."

"Boss, you are stupid. Let's settle for a standoff."

"You just lost a booze ration, Kwango. Tell him what I said."

113

Scolopen backed off a little, and signalled. A warrior dismounted. Ostentatiously, he removed his sword and dropped his battle-axe. Then he took off his armour and his helmet, and stepped forward.

Conrad put down his laser rifle. He stepped down from the platform and went towards the gate.

Before he opened the gate, he called Lieutenant Smith on his transceiver. "As of now, and until I return, you are in command, Lieutenant. You are to avoid offensive action until or unless the safety of the vessel is at risk."

"Just what the hell are you doing?" she demanded.

"I'm going to take out the big guy who had fun with Hildegarde."

"You are in no shape for that sort of idiotic gesture."

"Most of me isn't," he admitted. "But you can run all day with your tin legs if you have to—and I can crack skulls all day with my tin arm. Over and out."

Conrad opened the stockade gate, stepped out, and closed it carefully.

He would not have admitted it to Lieutenant Smith, but he was feeling bloody awful. Exhaustion was catching up with him again. The tension was taking its toll. His eyesight wavered, and the sky seemed to darken momentarily. He shook his head and walked resolutely towards the big Zelosian. He was aware that his gait was none too steady but he hoped nobody would notice.

The Zelosian was at least a head taller than Conrad. His shoulders were correspondingly broad, and the muscles on his arms and legs bulged. Conrad surveyed him with grudging admiration. He was in perfect physical condition.

Then Conrad glanced at Hildegarde Dolfuss, bruised and battered, tied to her frame. He moved away from the Zelosian and took a few steps towards her.

"Can you hear me, Hildegarde?"

She lifted up her head. Her face was badly battered, there were blood stains on her chin, her eyes were puffy, and one was completely closed. There were marks on her arms and legs where, presumably, she had been held, and there was massive bruising on her belly and thighs. Conrad was appalled.

She managed to speak. He could barely catch the words. "Sorry I disobeyed orders, Commander. Have I made a mess of things?"

"Not to worry, love." Conrad's voice was gentle. "You'll be with friends in a few minutes."

While he was exchanging those few words with Dolfuss, Scolopen had made further utterance, and the Zelosian captain was laughing.

Kwango gave the translation over the loud-hailer. "Scolopen wants to know if you will take the woman and retire from the contest. He says you don't walk too steady and, from where he sits, it looks as if his captain, who is twice your weight, is going to hammer you into the ground."

A black rage surged through Conrad. Adrenalin pulsed through him and annihilated all awareness of fatigue and pain.

"Tell Scolopen to get two more of his tough-guy rapists ready for action. This boyo isn't going to take long."

"Boss, you're crazy!"

"So I am, Kwango. I don't like what these heroes did to Dolfuss. Make the signal."

While Kwango was talking, Conrad turned and walked towards the Zelosian captain. He stopped when he was three metres away. The Zelosian laughed at him.

"Come on, bastard," grated Conrad. "Come and collect."

But the Zelosian was apparently in the mood to make it an exhibition bout. He jumped up and down, beating his chest, flexing his muscles. With great speed and agility, he ran round Conrad several times—Conrad being compelled to turn constantly to face him.

"O.K., funny man," said Conrad, "this is your party." Rapidly, he bent down, pushed his prosthetic hand through the grass, felt the soil and let his fingers scoop up a large clod, complete with grass attached. Expertly, he threw it at the Zelosian's face. It connected. Conrad laughed.

The Zelosian didn't have the same sense of humour. He wiped the dirt from his face, and glared at Conrad with murderous hate.

"You look like garbage," said Conrad pleasantly. "Your

mother was a whore and your father had syphilis. Also, you have bad breath."

The Zelosian didn't understand, but he got the message that he was being insulted. With a great roar of anger, he sprang at Conrad.

He didn't connect.

The prosthetic arm came up in a blur of action that was too fast to be seen by all who watched.

The Zelosian was dead before he hit the ground. His throat was smashed to pulp, his neck was broken, and his head only remained attached to his body by a strip of skin at the back.

Conrad turned to face Kwango. "Make to Scolopen: Next, please. Also tell him I still wish to talk peace." Calmly, Conrad wiped his bloody prosthetic hand on the grass.

Kwango called back, "Score one, Boss. Scolopen says your bones are made of iron, and he does not wish to send more of his best men to certain death. But, if you demand it, others will face you, since none are cowards. He says that Conrad of the Silver Patch is a man of his word, and a great warrior. He will talk peace."

"Amen," said Conrad. "The show is over. Some people take a lot of convincing."

He left the dead Zelosian and walked to where Hildegarde was strapped to the frame. Six mounted Zelosians were close by. As he approached, they drew their swords.

Jesus! thought Conrad. Didn't they hear what their boss-man said? But he walked on resolutely.

Suddenly all six warriors raised the hilts of their swords to their chests so that the blades pointed upwards to the sky, flashing in the sunlight.

"*Di engraeo numas Daritza, sfy Daritza*", they shouted in unison. Then the flashing swords were lifted high and brought slowly down in flashing arcs until they rested by the warriors' sides, their blades pointing to the ground.

"Score two, Boss," called Kwango. "They salute you as a warrior of warriors."

Conrad did not answer. He climbed on the cart and started untying Hildegarde's bonds.

Scolopen spoke.

Kwango translated. "Score three, Boss. Scolopen says that salute is reserved only for kings and winners of the Games."

"Tell him I'm very happy, etcetera. Tell him I like his style and I think his bully boys are all good clean-living guys. . . . You know the sort of crap, Kwango."

"Yes, Boss, I know that sort of crap."

"Tell him also that I take my sister back. Then we talk peace."

Conrad loosed the bonds round Hildegarde's ankles. A Zelosian warrior dismounted and tried to help him. Conrad glared at the man, and he fell back.

"Can you walk, love?"

Hildegarde tried to smile. "You want me to walk, Commander, I can walk. I'm a bloody Expendable, aren't I?"

"Darn right, Dolfuss. You are a bloody Expendable." He lifted her down to the ground.

"I saw what you did to that man."

"He had it coming to him. I've seen what he and his friends did to you."

"Thanks, Commander."

Conrad scratched his eyepatch irritably. "O.K., Dolfuss, that is enough of sentiment. You may have been had by half the Zelosian army, but you are going to walk back to the stockade as if you were a queen."

Hildegarde laughed weakly. "A queen with a bare bottom."

But, somehow, she managed to straighten her back and hold her head high. Conrad took her by the hand.

Phase Two

CONRAD DOES IT AGAIN

Fortunately for Kwango and for Conrad—but for different reasons—Scolopen's further utterances were fairly brief.

Kwango's head was throbbing and aching with the effort of having to use a language he had only just begun to learn, and Conrad was out on his feet.

While the discussion went on, Lieutenant Smith unharnessed from her exo and took Dolfuss to the sick bay for examination and treatment. Hal Mencken stayed in harness and at the ready, just in case some Zelosian joker thought it would be amusing to toss another king-size baseball. But the Immortals were well-disciplined. There were no further signs of aggression.

Scolopen said, "Conrad of the Silver Patch, I know now that you are a man of honour and great power. You came to my land uninvited." He smiled faintly. "But, for a time, you will remain as my guest. The blood that has been shed cannot be unshed. But we will speak of that later. I return now to Rossvallin to pursue my duties and to prepare for the Games. I will leave with you two of my counsellors to instruct you and your people in our customs and our language." Again he smiled faintly. "It may be that we shall understand each other better when it is no longer necessary for the black-faced warrior to be your voice. Five days from now, a squadron of my Immortals will come to escort you and as many of your attendants as you require to Rossvallin. Then you will tell me why you came to this land. It is agreed?"

The effort of translation was now making Kwango sweat profusely. Great beads formed on his forehead and dripped down his face.

"Make back," said Conrad. "It is agreed. Scolopen, King and Emperor, speaks wisely, and is a great man."

"You sure you know what you're doing, Boss? This guy might try some very funny tricks if he gets you on his home territory."

"He won't. He has seen enough to convince him that we are pretty tough customers. Deliver the message, Kurt. Your agony is almost over."

Scolopen had one last question. He pointed to the *Santa Maria*. "This tower of metal—what is it? Is it a machine of war?"

No, Scolopen. It is the ship which has brought us from a world beyond the stars to this world of yours."

"A ship which has voyaged from beyond the stars. It does not seem possible, yet I know you are a man of your word. I will think on this, as will my counsellors. Meanwhile, Conrad, farewell until we meet again."

Scolopen gave a signal. All except two of his warriors drew back and formed into a column. With the exception of the shattered siege engine and the cart on which the helicopter was carried, all the other vehicles swung round. Slowly, Scolopen raised his hand towards Conrad. It looked like some kind of a formal salute, so Conrad emulated the gesture. Then Scolopen turned and rode to the head of the column.

Conrad looked at the two Zelosians who had been left behind. "Tell those characters to tether their longhorns or something, and ask them to come inside, Kurt. Then offer them some food and say you need to rest before doing any more talking. Tell 'em the robots and the exos won't harm them."

"O.K. Boss. This translation kick has ruined me for ever."

Conrad took up his transceiver. "I'll get Hal to look after them while you go pour yourself a stiff drink. You were good, Kurt. Without your effort, there would have been one hell of a mess."

"I am always good," said Kwango. "But occasionally superb. This was one of the occasions."

"Don't set it to music," said Conrad drily. "I'm not in the mood." He radioed Mencken. "Stand down, Hal. The show is over. I liked your style with the baseball."

"Thanks, Commander. How is Hildegarde?"

"She'll live. . . . Stand down everyone. Back to normal duty. The show is over. . . . Hal, when you have unharnessed, look after our guests while Kurt unscrambles his circuits."

"Hell, Commander, I don't know their lingo. How am I going to get through to them?"

"Try sign language. Try anything. But don't hit them. And don't take them into the ship. They are not ready for that."

While Kwango was talking to the Zelosians, Conrad went up to *Santa Maria*'s sick bay. Hildegarde Dolfuss was lying peacefully in bed with her eyes closed.

"I've given her a shot," said Lieutenant Smith. "She'll be out for a few hours."

"How is she?"

Lieutenant Smith gave him a wintry smile. "About as well as any victim of multiple rape and brutal assault."

Conrad passed his hand over his head wearily. "I'm sorry, love. It wasn't meant to be a stupid question."

Lieutenant Smith gazed at him in surprise. "You just called me love!"

Conrad tried to pull himself together. "Sorry again, Lieutenant. A slip of the tongue."

"I can remember a time when you had many such slips of the tongue," she said softly. "Applecross. What a wonderful place it was. The North West Highlands of Scotland were all that you promised."

"We'll go there again," he said. "When we have finished with this bloody planet. I know I've been driving you all very hard, but . . ." He paused. The deck seemed to be wobbling, and the world was darkening. "Indira, my love," he said thickly, "I think I've had it." He made one last effort to be sensible. "Lieutenant Smith, please assume command."

Indira tried to catch him as he fell, but she failed. He hit the deck with a crash, ruining all her fancy needlework. The stitches on his face burst, the wounds broke open, and blood poured out onto the deck.

Lieutenant Smith knelt by him, turned him on his back and began to wipe the blood away from his cheek. Tears she could not control fell from her eyes and mingled with the blood. She swore silently at herself, but the tears would not stop.

She looked down at the pale and bloodied face. There was even blood on the silver eye patch. Conrad was a mess.

"James Conrad," she sobbed, "you are the most stupid, obstinate, egotistical bastard I have ever known. Why the hell do I love you?"

Conrad made no response. He was out cold. Lieutenant Smith struggled to pull herself together. She checked heartbeat and respiration, and then she called Kwango.

"Come up to the sick bay, Kurt. Superman has just smashed himself up again."

Kwango said, "That man is a menace to all shipping. I was just enjoying a nice, relaxing drink at his expense. What has he done now?"

"He's fallen flat on his face, Kurt. He has ruined my needlework—probably on purpose. Prognosis is that he is not going to be much use to himself or anyone else for forty-eight hours."

Kwango whistled. "That man sure has an insatiable appetite for disaster."

"This man," said Lieutenant Smith, "is one hell of a man. He has already scored two for mankind. He is entitled."

"Yes, Lieutenant, he's entitled. I'll be with you pronto."

Phase Three

ORDERS TO SHOOT

Lieutenant Smith gave Conrad a shot that would keep him out for at least twenty-four hours. Then, patiently, she set to work, patching up his face yet again. Finally, she dripped half a litre of blood back into him. He looked as if he needed it.

When he finally woke up, he found that Jane Ustinov was sitting by his bed. She was a pretty little thing, he thought hazily. Not sexy in the way that the big, blonde, bosomy Hildegarde Dolfuss was sexy, but finely formed and rather intense. The long black hair made her face seem paler than it actually was. He remembered that on occasion he had seen her and Jean-Pierre Gautier exchanging significant glances. As he collected his wits, he wondered how long it would be before they requested permission to spend the night together.

Ustinov noticed that he was awake. "Welcome back, Commander. How are you feeling?"

That was a good question. Conrad felt his face cautiously. It was stiff and numb, but not too bad. Lieutenant Smith—bless her—had put it all back together and applied some more syntheskin.

"I'm O.K., Jane. How long have I been out?"

"A little less than thirty hours."

"Blast! What's been happening?"

"A lot. Hal has fixed the chopper. It's operational once more. Hildegarde is up and about. She still aches and the bruises look dreadful; but she is working in the lab. She wanted to. Lieutenant Smith thought it would take her mind off recent events. Kurt has spent a lot of time with the Zelosians—he says they have a fascinating culture—and we have all been taking a crash course in their dreadful language. Kurt has also run a lot of data on the ecosystem through the computer. He says the biosphere is almost identical to that of Terra before we fouled it up with too much technology and too many people. He says it may have been planned that way."

"Has the infallible Kwango been drinking?" enquired Conrad drily.

Jane Ustinov smiled. "Well, he got slightly smashed with Zetuko and Kimatun last night. He said it was in the course of duty."

"Did he?" Conrad raised an eyebrow. "And who authorized him to fill the natives with booze!"

"Lieutenant Smith. I think Kurt convinced her it would be good for interracial relations."

"It seems things are a little out of hand," said Conrad grimly. "I'll soon settle that. Get a robot to bring me my clothes and—"

"Commander," said Jane Ustinov. "You have not yet resumed command. I have orders to see that you stay in bed until Lieutenant Smith has examined you."

"As of now, those orders are countermanded. I will inform Lieutenant Smith that—"

Ustinov lifted a small anesthetic gun and pointed it at him. "I have been instructed to drop you if you make a move," she said pleasantly. "Don't make me do it. You'll wake up with a headache."

For a few moments, Conrad was speechless. Finally, he

said in a controlled voice, "Ustinov, have the goodness to call Lieutenant Smith and tell her to get here fast."

Before Ustinov could reply, Lieutenant Smith's voice came over the intercom. "I have an open channel on you, James Conrad. You have a history of troublemaking when you are in the sick bay. That is why you are under guard."

"Under guard!" he roared, forgetting about his face. Needles of pain went everywhere. He sank back on his pillow, sweating.

"I bet that hurt," said Lieutenant Smith. "Relax, mister —or I'll tell Ustinov to shoot you, anyway. I'm tired of stitching your face together. A robot is bringing you some soup. Drink it all. And no more nonsense. I'll examine you when I am ready."

"No more nonsense!" stormed Conrad, oblivious to the pain. "Dammit to hell, woman, I am in full possession of my faculties, and by virtue of the authority invested in me by—"

"You don't have any authority. You are just an injured man, and probably the worst patient I ever had. I am now the legal commander of this expedition. It is all in the log. I'll stand down only when or if I judge you fit to resume command . . . Ustinov, are you prepared to use the anagun?"

"Yes, Commander."

"Keep well clear of him, then. If he makes one suspicious move, shoot. Try to hit the chest or shoulder."

"Will do, Commander."

"Over and out."

The robot Mark brought the soup. Conrad tried again.

"Mark, remove the anagun with minimal force from Ustinov. She has threatened to use it on me. Then bring my day clothes. Execute!"

"Request noted, sir. Execution will proceed if decision confirmed by Commander Smith."

"You, too?" Conrad was appalled.

"Please amplify statement/question. I regret I have insufficient data.'"

"Cancel," said Conrad wearily, "and give me the bloody soup."

"Decision noted. Execution proceeds."

Conrad raised himself. At least, the soup smelled good. He realized he was hungry.

Jane Ustinov smiled. "Now you are being sensible, sir. Lieutenant Smith told me to tell you that you could only get your revenge at Applecross. What does that mean —or is it a private thing?"

"It's a private thing, Ustinov. And you know damn well that bitch is listening to all I say."

Indira's voice came over the intercom. "Conrad, you have just been fined one booze ration—for insubordination."

He wanted to laugh, but that wouldn't do his face much good. He wanted to say, I love you. But Ustinov was present and, hell, it wasn't the right time.

Se he just said: "Permission requested to talk to Kwango, Commander."

"Permission granted, Conrad—when you have finished the soup, when I have examined you, and when Mr. Kwango is available."

"Thank you, sir," he said with irony. "There will be compound interest to pay at Applecross."

Phase Four

A PROBLEM FOR TERRA

It was another hour before Lieutenant Smith came to examine Conrad. He tried to contain his impatience. He didn't succeed. But at least he managed not to lose his temper with her. And that was progress.

"Now can I get out of this damn bed?" he asked when she had finished her inspection.

She shook her head. "Pulse is still slightly weak, temperature a little high. You have driven yourself into the ground. You need to rest somewhat. But, if you behave yourself, you can get up for dinner this evening. How's that?"

He ignored the question. "When can I resume duty?"

"If you get a good night's sleep and your temperature comes down, I'll pass you as fit for light duty tomorrow."

"That means, I trust, that I can assume full command once more?"

Indira smiled. "No, it doesn't, James. It means that you can direct operations if you wish, but that you can't leave the *Santa Maria*, and that you will be subject to prescribed rest periods until you are pronounced fully fit. The rest of the team are prepared to back me up, so don't think you can divide and conquer. And if your condition deteriorates—back to the sick bay."

"Thank you—Commander," he said caustically. "May I now talk to Kurt?"

"I'll call him. I'll be back in about an hour. Kurt knows the score, so don't try anything. He, too, has orders to restrain you."

Conrad said, "Some day, you might even make a good commander."

Lieutenant Smith leaned over him and kissed his forehead lightly. "I doubt it, James. My main talent lies not in making decisions, but in picking up the pieces."

"It is a formidable talent," conceded Conrad. "Without you, I would have been dead some time ago. So you won't apply for an independent command?"

She ran a hand through her lovely white hair. "James Conrad, you are a bloody fool."

Kwango came a couple of minutes after Indira had gone.

"Boss, you look like Son of Frankenstein on a bad day. How are you feeling?"

"Like Son of Frankenstein on a bad day. What's the news, Kurt?"

"You won't like it too much, Boss. I been talking somewhat to the guys Scolopen left with us. My Zelosian improves hourly. That invite to Rossvallin was really an invite to the Games."

"So?"

"To take part, Boss," explained Kwango. "Since we

didn't have a shoot-out, and since we knocked off a few of their people, Scolopen figures they got to have a fair crack at us—their way, not ours. It has all got to do with prestige, status, image, losing face, or whatever you care to call it. Scolopen seems to have lost face when he didn't stamp us into the ground, as promised. His only way of getting back into the charts is to show the Zelosians that we are grreat warriors, to be respected and treated with honour."

"So, in fact, he now wants us to take out some more of his people?"

Kwango shrugged. "That's about it, Boss. Or preferably, vice versa. Those characters he left with us, Zetuko and Kimatun, think they are very subtle. They tell us how tough we are and how clever we are and how much the Zelosians would respect us if we knocked off a few of their heavies in fair combat."

"Or vice versa," said Conrad drily.

Kwango was silent for a few moments. Then he said, "Boss, I been thinking about the mission."

"That's what you are paid for."

"I been thinking we ought to get the hell out."

"Why?"

"Because there are people here."

"So?"

"So I know my history. I don't like what the white colonists did to the American Indian and the negro. These Zelosians are tough, but there aren't many of them. If we colonize, a hundred years from now they could be living on reservations, or enjoying the benefits of Social Security because they can't compete economically with robots."

Conrad raised himself up. "Kwango, I am not empowered to abort this mission because of a value judgement. I am only empowered to abort if the planet is unsuitable for human beings—demonstrably, it isn't—or if casualties, actual or anticipated, render the success of the mission impossible."

"We get mixed up in those War Games," said Kwango gloomily, "and you can abort under clause two."

"I don't think colonization need be disastrous for

126

these people," said Conrad. "There are only thousands of them on a planet that could support millions. They don't have or need much territory on this continent. We could settle on the land they don't need or want."

"That's it!" snorted Kwango. "The reservation mentality. You draw a line anywhere at all on the map and say: right, you folks, just stay north of the border; and you've put them in a reservation. No matter how big it is. Boss, this is *their* world."

"I'll thank you not to lecture me!" snapped Conrad acidly. "The whole of human history boils down to the conquest and development of new territories."

"For development, read exploitation."

"Also," went on Conrad, "I would remind you that evolution is based on the survival of the fittest."

"And who's to decide who's fittest? These people may have some peculiar notions, but they haven't exhausted their natural resources like we did on Terra."

"They haven't even touched them," said Conrad. "Anyway, the problem is not ours, Kurt. I'm going to toss it back to U.N. by subspace radio, and let the eggheads on Terra sort it out."

Kwango did some rapid calculations. "Twenty-four light years . . . It will be about seventy Z-days before you can get a reply. What do we do meanwhile?"

"We're Expendables. We continue to prove the planet, or bust ourselves trying . . . Now, call Matthew for me. The drain on the generators is going to be dreadful. He'll have to work out a programme of pulse transmissions. I think we can now cram about a hundred words into each one-second blast . . . And when you have done that, Kurt, write me a concise report on the entire situation—ecology, biosphere, analysis, culture level of the Zelosians, and whatever else is relevant. Try to keep it less than one thousand words."

"A report and recommendation?" asked Kwango hopefully.

"No. Just a report—which I will myself edit as necessary."

When Matthew came, Conrad said, "Make ready for sub-space radio transmission, six hours from now."

"Decision noted. Execution proceeds. What is the anticipated volume of transmission, sir?"

"Approximately one thousand words, English language, plus or minus ten percent. How long will such a transmission take?"

"Approximately eleven point two five seconds, sir, plus or minus ten percent, each pulse separated by thirty E-minutes, under standard safety procedure. If the situation is designated as an emergency, pulse intervals may be reduced to—"

"The situation is not designated as an emergency. Use normal procedure."

"Decision noted. Execution proceeds."

Phase Five

MIND THE STORE!

By the time the squadron of Immortals had arrived to escort Conrad to Rossvallin, much had happened. He had recovered his strength rapidly, and Lieutenant Smith had relinquished command as she had promised.

The report Kwango had drafted was exactly nine hundred and fifty words long. It was entirely factual, and the data had been brilliantly compressed. But that was what one expected of Kwango, thought Conrad. The black man had a compulsion to excel in practically every damn thing. Not one word of the report needed to be changed. The generators of the *Santa Maria* yielded the necessary energy required for the subspace radio blasts, but by the time the sequence finished, the cooling systems were almost at danger level.

Hildegarde Dolfuss seemed cheerful enough when Conrad talked to her. She blamed no one but herself for what had happened. She had ventured just that little bit too far and had been ambushed by a couple of Zelosian scouts. She obviously didn't want to talk about what had happened after that and, wisely, Conrad did not press her.

Zetuko and Kimatun, the counsellors Scolopen had left with the Expendables, were huge and well-built men by Earth standards, but lightly built by Zelosian standards. However, being Immortals, they were obviously veteran warriors. Conrad took a crash course in Zelosian so that he could talk to them directly.

Kwango gave him his first lessons, and took a certain malicious pleasure when lines of fatigue appeared on Conrad's face and his head began to ache with concentration. Kwango was taking his revenge for the tremendous effort that had been required of him at the confrontation with Scolopen—and Conrad knew it.

"Want to rest, Boss?" asked Kwango with mock concern. "I told you their syntax was hell."

"No, thanks," said Conrad evenly. "Proceed. It's harder than German but easier than Russian. I'll live through it."

Having had his fun, Kwango relented and put a half dozen programmed lessons on tape for the sleep-teach machine. Lieutenant Smith gave Conrad a shot of hypnolax, and in four hours he woke up from a twilight sleep, feeling slightly dazed, but with a good command of Zelosian.

When he had recovered his wits, he talked to Zetuko and Kimatun. To his surprise, they turned out to be highly intelligent men. They had already assimilated the basic concept of robotics and the function of exoskeletons, and they accepted that the *Santa Maria* was a vessel that had brought Conrad and his companions from a world beyond the sky. The knowledge had not reduced them to a state of cultural shock. Conrad detected the hidden hand of Kwango. He had done a good P.R. job.

Conrad thought long and hard about who should go to Rossvallin. The main problem was: would Scolopen try anything funny either at the *Santa Maria* or in Rossvallin? He thought not, but he was not prepared to take too much of a gamble. In the end, he decided to leave Hal Mencken and Hildegarde Dolfuss, along with all the robots, to mind the store. Hal was good with an exo, and if the stockade were attacked, Hildegarde had only to push buttons to blow the mines. Matthew could stand permanent watch at the command screens, and one robot would be needed in the ship for maintenance and service, but the remainder could patrol endlessly if required. So the stockade should be safe, even if Scolopen or one of his captains tried to get clever.

It followed that the party going to Rossvallin was at greater risk. He intended that they should all be armed with laser rifles and small anaguns. Such things would be effective if they were at a distance from the enemy. But if they were closely surrounded by friends, who suddenly took it into their heads to become enemies, such weapons were virtually useless. Still, the risk had to be taken. Some kind of understanding or arrangement with Scolopen had to be reached, in order to avoid any future confrontation.

The squadron of Immortals, about a hundred mounted warriors, waited patiently outside the stockade, drawn up in two columns, while Conrad gave last minute instructions to Matthew, Hal, and Hildegarde.

"Matthew, I want you to post Luke, John, Peter and Paul outside the stockade, north, south, east, west, at a distance of one kilometre. They are to maintain radio contact with you every fifteen minutes, and they are to advise you of the approach of any of the beings now designated as Zelosians. The robots are to be armed with laser rifles, for use only in the event of an attack. If an attack is mounted, all robots will return to the stockade and take up their assigned defensive positions. You will also maintain the *Santa Maria* ready for emergency lift-off. During my absence, Mr. Mencken is in command. You will obey his commands, even if counter to my own."

"Decisions noted," Matthew replied efficiently. "Execution proceeds."

Conrad turned to Mencken. "Hal, it's basically a holding operation. I don't think you will have any trouble, but I'm not betting. Don't take chances. After we leave, one of us will call you every hour on the hour, night and day. If you don't get a call for three consecutive hours, assume something nasty has happened."

"In which case, Commander, I'll harness up into an

exo and come and stamp their town flat until I find you, while Hildegarde burns them from the chopper."

"No!" snapped Conrad. "We are not here to commit genocide, no matter what the provocation. If those of us who are going to Rossvallin get smashed, you will lift-off, get back to Terra and supply ExPEND with all available data. Let them decide what, if anything, to do. Understood?"

Mencken shrugged. "Understood, Commander. But I don't have to like it."

"Hildegarde, how are you feeling?" Conrad was gentle, solicitous. Her bruises had faded, but she still looked pale and withdrawn.

"Don't worry about me, James. I'm fine."

Conrad wondered if he ought to reprimand her for calling him James, then decided against it.

"You can cope?"

"Try me."

Conrad smiled. "I'm doing just that. . . . O.K., you two. Mind the store. We'll be back as soon as we can."

Impulsively, Hildegarde kissed him full on the lips. She pressed her body close. Conrad was instantly excited by her intense sexuality.

"That will cost you one booze ration, Dolfuss," he managed to say, gently extricating himself from her arms.

"It was worth it," said Hildegarde. "Just come back in one piece."

Phase Six

SCOLOPEN'S EAR

The journey to Rossvallin was accomplished with remarkable speed—far faster than Conrad would have thought possible. He had anticipated that it would have to be done in two stages, but the entire hundred kilometres was covered in one day, with one stop only. The party arrived at Rossvallin more than an hour before sunset.

Two huge double-wheeled chariots had been provided for the "comfort" of the visitors. The wheels were wooden, and more than two metres in diameter. Each had a thick flexible tyre made of some substance obviously similar to Terran rubber. Each chariot was drawn by a team of six longhorns—which the Zelosians called pulpuls—controlled by a single charioteer.

The floors of the massive chariots were lined with thick layers of the same rubbery substance. Animal skins had been laid over the rubber for the comfort of Scolopen's guests. Conrad, Ustinov and Gautier travelled in one chariot, together with the counsellor Zetuko, while Lieutenant Smith, Kwango and Kimatun rode in the other.

The two columns set off at a cracking pace, with the chariots in the rear. Conrad estimated the speed at about thirty kilometres an hour. He did not think the beasts would be able to keep that up for long.

The chariots lurched about crazily as the huge wheels passed over the uneven ground. Despite the tyres and the floor padding, it was necessary to hold on firmly to the side of the vehicle to avoid being thrown about. Conrad noticed that Zetuko and the charioteer rarely needed to use handholds. They were like experienced sailors on a heaving deck. The charioteer used his whip frequently and shouted Zelosian oaths, presumably to encourage the pulpuls.

The landscape sped by. Conrad looked back and could just see sunlight glinting on the top of the *Santa Maria* in the distance. He waved to Lieutenant Smith, whose chariot was about five metres away. Her white hair was streaming in the wind and her finely formed brown face wore an expression of exhilaration.

"How do you like the buggy ride, Lieutenant?" he called.

"It's fine. I just hope we don't break our necks."

Gautier seemed very pale. "I think I am going to be sick, Commander."

"Permission denied," snapped Conrad. "Take a pill and sip some water." He turned to Zetuko, and spoke in halting Zelosian. "How long can your pulpuls keep up this pace, Zetuko?"

"Lord, they will run until they burst their hearts, if we require it. But that is not necessary, as you will see."

Gautier took a pill from his med kit and sipped some water from his canteen. He still didn't look too good, but at least he wasn't sick. Jane Ustinov comforted him. Presently, he began to recover.

The chariots splashed through streams and lurched over the rolling ground, with hardly any slackening of pace. But after a couple of hours, a warrior at the head of each column gave a signal, and the pulpuls slowed down to a kind of fast trot.

Eventually, by a small stream-fed lake in a large stretch of relatively flat ground, the party came upon two more columns of Immortals and two more chariots, drawn up and ready, facing north.

"My Lord Conrad," said Zetuko, "it is now necessary that we make use of fresh beasts, while these that have served us well take their ease." He glanced at Gautier. "It may be that you and your companions will wish to take food and wine and rest. The remainder of the journey is as much as we have travelled thus far."

"What about it, Jane, Jean-Pierre?" asked Conrad. "Would you like a break?"

"I'm all right now, Commander," gulped Gautier.

"I would like a short break, Commander," said Jane.

Conrad turned to the Zelosian. "Zetuko, we will rest briefly. Also, we will take a little food and wine."

Zetuko bowed his head. "It shall be."

Incredibly thin slices of meat were served on wooden platters. Metal goblets, probably silver, were filled with a chilled white wine. The meat reminded Conrad of the thin slices of raw reindeer meat he had once eaten at a party back on Terra, in Stockholm, Sweden. It had a piquant flavour, not unpleasing. The wine tasted like a good Hock. He wondered how they had managed to chill it.

Kwango said, "These people got a nice line in *hors d'oeuvre,* Boss." He licked his fingers—no cutlery had been offered—and expertly dropped another strip of meat into his mouth. "Maybe they ain't so stupid as we thought."

Then came the big surprise. Kimatun said in perfect English, "Kwango, I am glad the meat is pleasing to your taste. It is the flesh of the pulpul."

Kwango gazed at him, speechless. Finally he collected his wits. "How did you do that?"

"I am a reader of minds. While you were learning our tongue, I journeyed among your thoughts, seeking the words of your tongue. I learned also."

"Did you do this with Kwango only?" asked Conrad. He could feel a cold sweat on his forehead. He had underestimated these warlike people. Damn!

"No, Lord Conrad. With others also, yourself included." He shrugged. "Scolopen bade me learn. I heard my king and obeyed."

"Are there many like you on this world?" asked Lieutenant Smith.

"Not many, my Lady. We are Scolopen's ears."

"So you know all about us," said Conrad heavily. He was thinking that pretty soon there would be a few dead Expendables in Rossvallin. Then he tried to cancel the thought—for obvious reasons.

"I know what it is needful to know," said Kimatun. "Fear not for your safety, Lord Conrad. You are the king's guests."

Before Conrad could reply, Zetuko said, "My lord, if you have rested and eaten, all is ready. Scolopen, King and Emperor, awaits the pleasure of your company."

Phase Seven

THE SAND RUNS THROUGH THE GLASS

Rossvallin looked far more imposing from the ground than it had done from the air. But though the Zelosians used stone for their city walls and for important buildings, they had not yet developed masonry to a great degree. The massive stone blocks they used were roughly cut, and there was little sign of any decoration or embellishment.

The route to the palace was lined with warriors, each of whom gave the royal salute as Conrad's chariot passed. Behind the lines of warriors, the population stood and stared. There were no cheers, no rumblings of disapproval or enmity, no raised fists or weapons. They just stood and stared. The women, Conrad noted, were poorly dressed. They kept glancing nervously at their menfolk, as if seeking guidance for their behavior. They were very obviously second-class citizens, used by the warrior caste, as Kwango had said, for pleasure, breeding and work.

Scolopen came down the steps of his palace to greet the Expendables. "Welcome, Conrad of the Silver Patch." His eyes flickered briefly towards Kwango and Gautier, Lieutenant Smith and Jane Ustinov. "Welcome also to your warriors and your women."

"Scolopen, King and Emperor, Triple Winner of the Games," said Conrad in adequate Zelosian, "I thank you. We have much to talk about."

Scolopen nodded his head gravely. "There will be a time for talking before we banquet. Tomorrow, Conrad, the Games begin. Some will carouse this night, having seen their last sunset. . . . Rooms have been prepared for you. Bathe and refresh yourselves. Then you and I will talk."

Kimatun spoke rapidly to the king—so rapidly that none of the Expendables could understand what he was saying.

Scolopen smiled. "My counsellor has many wonders to report. I will hear what he has to say. Then we will discuss these matters further."

"How is your son, Orylos?"

"Let us not speak of Orylos. It is my wish."

"Then, Scolopen, I will respect your wish." Conrad was puzzled.

The king gave a command, and the Expendables were escorted into the great palace, through a large hall, and up a rough, stone staircase to their chambers.

The rooms were very simply furnished. Tapestries hung on the stone walls; the beds were thick mattresses lying on the floor, covered with cushions and skins; the windows were high and narrow, the glass thick and distorted. Each chamber had its own bath, sunken into the stone floor. Warm water constantly bubbled through a hole in the bottom of the bath, and the surplus water constantly discharged through an overflow hole a little below the rim. The floors felt warm to the touch, and the steady bubbling of the water was a soothing sound.

"Boss," said Kwango, "these people ain't stupid. I think they have tapped hot springs or artesian wells."

"Very likely" said Conrad. "It's about time I called Hal again." He reached for his transceiver. "Tell the others that if anyone wants to have a bath, they can do so only if another Expendable with laser rifle at the ready is present."

Kwango grinned. "You worry too much. I'll stand guard over Lieutenant Smith, Boss."

"Alas, Kurt, I'm sure she would prefer Ustinov."

Each Expendable had been assigned two female servants. They were big, shapely women with long blonde hair. They were barefoot and simply dressed, and they kept their eyes downcast. They spoke only when spoken to.

Conrad was the only one who decided not to bathe. He joined Gautier, who was standing guard, while Kwango amused himself in the endless flow of warm water.

"What do you think of Rossvallin, Jean-Pierre?"

Gautier shrugged. "It is heavy, oppressive. Without refinement—like the people who built it. These people—what do they know of culture? All they know about—all they think about—is violence. Unlike Kurt, I would like to see Zelos colonized and these people pacified."

"Better not let Kimatun catch you expressing such sentiments."

Gautier laughed. "In his presence, Commander, I now think and give voice only to beautiful thoughts. Still, I would like to have the mystery of their origin solved. They are as we are. It is amazing. Theoretically, it should be impossible."

"I got an explanation, Boss," said Kwango, sprawling indolently in the water. "If you'd like to hear the Kwango scenario—"

"Save it!"

Kimatun had just entered the chamber. "Lord Conrad, I came from Scolopen, King and Emperor, who awaits your company, having that to say which is for your ears only."

Conrad turned to Gautier. "I was just about to call the *Santa Maria*. It's about time. Call for me and tell Hal all goes well."

Then he said to Kimatun, "I am anxious to speak with the great and wise Scolopen."

Kimatun glanced at the laser rifle slung over Conrad's shoulder. "My Lord, it would be greatly appreciated if you did not bring your fire-weapon. In his own palace Scolopen does not bear arms, and you are his honoured guest."

"The King's warriors bear arms," said Conrad. "We are few. They are many."

"Lord, forgive me. You do not know the ways of our people. To kill an unarmed man merits such punishment that even the most brave are deterred. Who touches you, touches Scolopen, for you are under the King's mantle. No man in the realm wishes to swallow his own dung before he is allowed to die.

Conrad tossed his laser rifle to Gautier. "If harm comes to me, burn the entire palace and all in it. Then burn Rossvallin and go back to the *Santa Maria*."

All of which was quite impossible, as Gautier knew and as Kwango knew. But Conrad gambled that Kimatun, wily as he was, would not know it.

Kimatun smiled. "The Lord Conrad is formidable."

"Take me to Scolopen."

The King's private apartment was small and comfortable. Scolopen sat on a high-backed wooden chair. A similar chair, though smaller, was provided for Conrad. He would have to look up at the King. He was amused at the gambit. Maybe the Zelosians thought they were being subtle.

"Leave us, Kimatun."

The counsellor bowed and withdrew.

"So, Conrad of the Silver Patch. I have learned that

you now speak enough of our language to understand my words. It is true?"

"It is true, Scolopen."

"I have learned many other things also. Kimatun has strange powers. They are useful."

"That, *I* have learned," said Conrad. "We did not know he could enter our thoughts."

Scolopen smiled. "It is well that we savages have some skills to set against your magic. I will speak plainly. Though it is hard to believe, I know that you have truly voyaged from beyond the stars, that you have many skills and machines that, to us, seem like things of magic. Indeed, the priests of Vallin say that you are demons come among us in human form." He shrugged. "But such is the way of priests when they are faced with powers greater than their own. Be that as it may, your purpose in coming to our world is to bring many of your own kind, to live here forever, building cities and growing strong."

"That was the reason we came," admitted Conrad.

"There are too many people on your world, Conrad."

"Yes. And there are not enough on yours."

Scolopen sighed. "But this is *our* world, Conrad. Because of your fearful weapons and greater numbers, in the end your people would take it from us, and my race would perish. Victory goes to the strong. We are strong in our bodies and our courage, but not in skills such as yours."

"Scolopen, we do not wish to make war on you. There is more than enough land for us all. The colonists could settle on land many, many days' travel away. There need be no strife or bloodshed."

"Would that be so for all time? I think not. The strong conquer the weak. That is the law of life." He smiled. "I know that, apart from the robots, you are only seven. Five of you are here in Rossvallin. It would be possible to have you killed. You have your fire-weapons, and many Immortals would die. Yet it would be possible."

"I thought the King's guests had the King's protection—on his word of honour."

"That is so," agreed Scolopen innocently. "But when

you leave Rossvallin, you will cease to be my guests."
He laughed. "Fear not, Conrad. I keep my word. Also,
if you were to die, others would come. And perhaps many
of your giants would demand an accounting."

"I wish to make an agreement with you—an agreement
that binds both our peoples to remain at peace with each
other."

Scolopen said, "Kwango, the black man, does not wish
your people to come to this land. He has told you so."

Conrad was startled. "Kimatun?"

Scolopen nodded gravely. "Even so. The ear of Scolopen. Did you think I would leave with you men who would
only teach and not learn?"

Conrad laughed. "You are a great general, Scolopen."

"It is true also that you have sent a message—how, I
know not—to the wise men of your world. You have told
them of our land and of our ways and customs. You have
asked their advice. How long before they answer, Conrad?"

"Sixty days at the earliest. Perhaps longer."

Scolopen sighed. "It is too long. You cannot make a
treaty that will endure with a dead king, Conrad. It may
be that I have already seen my last sunset—as has Orylos,
my son, without doubt. The next king will lead not only
the Immortals but every man who can bear arms against
you."

"Scolopen, I beg you to explain this thing. I do not
understand."

"When you returned my son to me, there were those
who whispered, muttered, talked. They saw that he was
alive and unwounded, and they said that his heart had
become as a woman's heart. When I did not destroy you,
there were other whisperings, other secret words. I, a
triple Winner of the Games, now also have the heart
of a woman." He gave a grim laugh. "Tomorrow, at
dawn, the Games begin. They continue till the sun sinks
over the arena. Orylos defends his manhood by entering
against the Mortal Three. In turn, he must defeat wrestler,
axeman and swordsman. Few survive against the Mortal
Three. It is, by custom, a way to die honourably. It is
a way to atone for dishonour."

"Orylos will defeat the wrestler," predicted Conrad confidently.

"Why do you say that?"

"He has learned new tricks, Scolopen. Kwango was his teacher."

"I thank you for that. With axe and sword, he has some skill. But even if Orylos should survive, it is less sure that I will. The Winner of the Games has the right of challenge. When a King and Emperor is respected by his people, the Winner rarely makes the challenge. But, since your coming, the mood of my people has changed. There is a man, Haruken, of great valour, of great strength, and in his prime. Also he has some subtlety of mind. He has entered only for those events which will lead him to the final combat. If he should win—and I think he may—he will challenge. Even if I should kill him, though youth and vigour are on his side, it will then be even harder to make peace between your people and mine. Haruken speaks openly of war to the death, and he is idolized. If I kill him, they will say that I am in league with you Outlanders and that I borrowed your magic. . . . I have told you these things because I know that your race has great power and can destroy my people if it chooses. Perhaps it is a jest of the gods than Haruken seeks to be the instrument of their destruction and is honoured for his avowed aims."

"Scolopen, I thank you for your honesty. You are a wise man, and one whom I have quickly learned to respect. There may yet be a way out of this dilemma. I will think about it."

Scolopen gave a grim laugh. "Think quickly, then, Conrad of the Silver Patch. The sand runs through the glass. Presently, we feast. Tomorrow, the Games."

Phase Eight

THE MORTAL THREE

It was half an hour before daybreak, Conrad estimated, and already the seats of the great amphitheatre had been filled. Conrad was sitting to the right of Scolopen, as an honoured guest. Immediately below him, Lieutenant Smith, Kwango, Gautier and Ustinov were perched on the stone seats accorded to most favoured persons.

The light of a thousand torches made the arena dance with eerie shadows. It was as though the ghosts of warriors long dead had returned briefly to enact their final moments yet again. The atmosphere was heavy with tension and anticipation. Presently, as the sun rose, the torches would be extinguished, and the death-or-glory ritual would begin.

As he waited, Conrad reviewed the events of the last few hours. The conversation he had had with Scolopen was still fresh in his mind. There had to be a solution to the problem, but he did not yet know what it was.

The feast of the preceding evening, held in the great hall of the palace, had been a fairly riotous, fairly friendly affair, with much strong wine and many toasts. But Conrad had sensed the undercurrents of tension. Haruken, the king's chief captain, had been present. He possessed, as Scolopen had said, great subtlety of mind. Every toast he made, every sentence he uttered carried a double meaning. He was a big, brawny man with huge shoulders, a coarse face, and thick lips, but a nimble tongue. He welcomed the Outlanders who, he said, were people of strange powers and perhaps some valour. He went on to say that perhaps Orylos, the king's son, had benefitted in peculiar ways from their company. He even ventured the thought that Scolopen, in view of his advancing years and great experience, had judged it wise to treat the

Outlanders as friends and honoured guests—even though blood had already been shed. This, concluded Haruken, was surely a supreme example of the wisdom of Scolopen.

The King did not deign to reply to these barbs, for that would have been to admit that Haruken had angered him.

But Conrad could not resist some retaliation. He got to his feet and raised his glass. "I drink to Haruken," he said. "I am told he is a great warrior, though I have not seen him fight. Certainly, he has skill with words. I drink to his skill with words, and wish him good luck in the Games. In my country, we have dogs who bark well and dogs who bite well. Tomorrow, we shall see if Haruken bites as well as he barks."

There were roars of laughter, followed by a sudden silence.

Haruken stood up and glared at Conrad. "You little know the ways of our land, Conrad of the Silver Patch," he snarled. "Were this not the King's palace, steel would flash and blood would flow to quench that insult."

Conrad had affected surprise. "Haruken, I am sorry if I have offended you. Perhaps it is that I speak your language ill. I do not wish to anger a great warrior who is so loyal to his King." Conrad raised his glass yet again.

The sarcasm seemed to have gotten through to Haruken. He fingered his belt nervously, as if seeking a weapon that was not there. He stared about him angrily—though no one would meet his gaze. Finally, he flexed his muscles and said, "There will be a reckoning, Outlander."

There were gasps at his insolent disregard for Conrad's now official title. Conrad rewarded him with a pleasant smile. "Good health, Haruken. Tomorrow, I will note how well you bite."

Shortly after that, Scolopen got up from his throne-like chair, signalling that the feast was over.

He went with Conrad some way to his chamber. "You have made an enemy to the death, Conrad. Haruken will not rest until he has killed you. There can now be little hope of peace between our peoples."

"Scolopen, I have only made an enemy of the enemy of peace. Is that not so?"

Scolopen smiled. "You play a dangerous game."

Conrad shrugged. "It appears to be my habit."

The night had passed without incident. Lieutenant Smith and Ustinov had shared the same chamber and had taken turns to stand watch. Gautier and Kwango had done similarly, also ensuring that regular contact with the *Santa Maria* was maintained. Conrad slept like a baby. Now and again, Kwango took a look at him. The Commander lay on his back, laser rifle firmly clutched in his prosthetic hand, entirely relaxed. In the flickering candlelight, the scars on his face were almost invisible. He looked like a young man.

But now, as he sat by Scolopen's side, waiting for the first rays of the sun to penetrate the gloom of the amphitheatre, Conrad did not feel at all like a young man. He felt old and tired, and his face was twitching where the wound was healing. If what Scolopen said was true, all Conrad's scheming would be in vain.

The first rays of the sun crept over the top of the amphitheatre, hitting a large concave mirror of polished metal at the far end of the arena. The mirror became a blaze of red fire and the beam of light was reflected across the arena. It illuminated the figure of a single warrior trumpeter, who stood on a great block of stone, turning him also into a thing of fire.

He raised the trumpet to his lips. As the fanfare rolled across the amphitheatre, the light intensified, and the thousand torches were extinguished. Before the trumpeter had stopped playing, the red light of the sun began to brighten the arena. It was filled by warriors and competitors drawn up in ranks.

They raised their arms in salute to Scolopen, and simultaneously shouted a word that Conrad did not know. The word was repeated by the audience, packed densely on the descending rings of seats.

Scolopen rose to speak. "We are met here to test the manhood of our people, to settle disputes in honourable fashion, to display valour, and to show joyfully that we know how to live and die. Many will be gathered up by the arms of Vallin before the sun sets this day. We shall rejoice at their passing to the Halls of the Brave, and to

Kwango sighed. "Yes, Boss. I just hope none of us has to waste our return tickets to dear old Terra."

The "popcorn" consisted of crisply fried balls of pulpul meat and the "coke" was chilled wine, supplied by women servants.

The battle had commenced. Conrad watched it intently. The contestants advanced warily upon each other. He noted that each man appeared to carry at least three weapons. The men of Orovallin seemed to favour the javelin, the morningstar and the sword. The men of Norvallin preferred the battle-axe. Presumably they all carried daggers.

The two opposing teams advanced to within ten metres of each other. Then javelins were hurled and battle-axes expertly thrown. Two of Orovallin fell to battle-axes, three of Neovallin fell to javelins. With great cries, the survivors rushed at each other, brandishing their remaining weapons.

The resulting carnage was brief, bloody, barbaric.

The single survivor, minus a hand, and with blood flowing from a dreadful stomach wound, managed to raise his good arm to Scolopen before he fell unconscious, probably to die soon after.

"The water rights to the river Suros are granted to Orovallin," said Scolopen calmly, "until such time as they are again disputed."

Two wagons drawn by pulpuls came into the arena. The dead were placed on one and the wounded and the dying on another. Conrad saw that only three men were laid on the wagon for the wounded.

"It was a good fight, was it not, Conrad?" said Scolopen.

"They were great warriors," acknowledged Conrad carefully.

Scolopen smiled. "Yet none of them was good enough for the Immortals."

Indira turned and said angrily in English: "My God, what savage butchery!"

Before Conrad could say anything, the voice of Kimatun came from behind Scolopen—also in English, "Not butchery, My Lady. They died as warriors, not as cattle."

Scolopen turned to Conrad. "Does the Lady Indira have no stomach for our Games. It is not surprising. As you see, our women do not watch the Games. They remain below only to receive the dead and the wounded."

"The Lady Indira dislikes only to see good men die," explained Conrad quietly. "Small though she is, she, too, is ranked as an Immortal in the world from which we came. She has the gift of speed. Before the sun sets today, some of your greatest athletes will look on her and be ashamed."

Scolopen raised an eyebrow. "A woman has never yet entered the Games. Women do not compete with men. They cannot."

Conrad shrugged. "I speak the truth, as you have seen. We shall compete in the Games. Was that not what you desired?"

Scolopen said: "Conrad, you are brave, that I know. You are also very wise or very foolish. Which, I do not know."

"There is only one way to find out, is there not?"

Scolopen did not reply.

While this exchange was going on, the arena had been cleared, sand had been sprinkled over the bloodstains, and an event that was a mixture of wild west rodeo and Spanish bullfight was now in progress. It was a non-mortal event—theoretically. Two men had already been gored to death as, bare-chested, they attempted to throw the wild pulpuls that had been driven into the arena. The trick was to grasp the horns of the charging pulpul, hang on for dear life, wait until the beast had been slowed down, then jerk the horns, twisting the neck so that the pulpul had to fall on its side. But, if the pulpul jerked first, disaster followed.

The morning wore on, the sun rose high. Mortal event followed non-mortal event. Individual combat, non-mortal, was followed by individual combat, to the death.

Then came the event which Scolopen secretly dreaded —the Mortal Three. It was, Conrad later learned, a most curious event. It was an event in which men condemned to death for various reasons could earn a pardon; in which a poor Zelosian could win wealth, land, women;

in which a man who no longer wished to live could achieve a spectacular suicide; and in which a man whose courage was in question could demonstrate—usually at the cost of his life—that he had, in fact, more courage than most.

The Mortal Three—the wrestler, the axeman and the swordsman—were men who had been condemned for such crimes as murder, treason, stealing another man's woman or women, or disobeying a royal command. If one of them were killed by one contestant, another condemned man would take his place. If one of them triumphed over a challenger, he was automatically granted his life but, was required to remain in the contest and face successive challengers.

This year, there were four challengers: Orylos, who sought to prove his courage; Anyako, who had been caught cheating at cards; Orovin, who had lost all his possessions at gaming; and Vostylag, whose women mocked his impotence. Each challenger was allowed to choose the order in which he would meet the Mortal Three. The order of challenge was decided by the drawing of lots.

The herald announced the event.

"Three dead men now enter this arena and, being dead, are nameless. Their crimes were grievous. Yet these Mortal Three, justly condemned by Scolopen, King and Emperor, may yet win back their lives. In the order of challenge, they are opposed by Orovin, son of Kosta; Vostylag, son of Menug; Orylos, son of Scolopen; Anyako, son of Tostig. Let Vallin judge the virtue of those who are about to live or die."

The Mortal Three took up their positions at the far end of the arena, each of them about twenty metres from his neighbour. Orovin, the first challenger, entered the arena from the other end. He was armed with axe and sword, but he wore no armour. His torso was bare.

He marched boldly up to the Mortal Three and inspected each of them carefully. Then he stood back and laid down his axe. He approached the swordsman and flourished his sword in salute. The salute was answered. Then the two men moved in close.

It was over very quickly. Orovin had miscalculated. The swordsman was good. After a few feints, he sheared Orovin's head off with a tremendous blow. The crowd roared. The body of Orovin, and his head, was quickly removed.

Vostylag, the next challenger, fared little better. He chose the axeman first, and defeated him with a lucky blow. The axeman, minus an arm, was wheeled away, and a new axeman took his place.

Vostylag then chose to wrestle. For a minute or two it seemed that he might have a chance. But the wrestler, a powerful and much heavier man, managed to get a firm hold. He threw Vostylag into the air and, as the unfortunate challenger came down, expertly raised a knee to break his back. Vostylag fell, writhing, and was carried off, still writhing in agony.

"I could fix that man," said Lieutenant Smith. "Let me go and—"

"Permission denied!" snapped Conrad.

"I want to be sick," said Jane Ustinov.

"Permission denied! You are an Expendable."

Orylos came into the arena. Conrad gazed at Scolopen. The King's expression seemed blank, but he leaned forward intently. Slowly, Orylos walked toward the Mortal Three. He inspected them carefully. The axeman was huge, even by Zelosian standards. He was perhaps ten centimetres taller than Orylos.

"That axeman is formidable," observed Gautier.

"The bigger they come, the harder they fall," said Kwango. "I taught that boy some very fancy footwork. I hope he remembers to use it. Anyway, he'll take the wrestler first, the swordsman second and that dynosaur last."

"How do you know?" asked Conrad.

Kwango looked pained. "The wrestler is three or four kilos lighter than Orylos. Also, he has not benefitted from the Kwango technique. The swordsman is about the same weight as Orylos, but he, too, doesn't know about fancy footwork. By the time Orylos has dealt with those two, the dynosaur is going to be worried. Good strategy. . . . Boss, I bet you a booze ration Orylos is the only one to walk out of this arena."

"Kurt, I will not bet on a man's life. But if it works out like that, you drink as much as you can hold, at my expense."

Kimatun hastily translated this exchange for Scolopen. He turned to Conrad. "If it comes to pass as the Lord Kwango has said, I, Scolopen, will make him as my brother. If I die—as may happen—he will inherit my lands, my cattle and my women."

Conrad said, "Kwango seeks no reward. Your son is his friend."

It was as Kwango had predicted. Orylos chose the wrestler first. The two men moved around each other warily.

"Make it fast, Orylos!" shouted Kwango in Zelosian. "You need your strength for the others."

Perhaps Orylos heard. Perhaps not.

The wrestler lunged, impatient to come to grips. Orylos rewarded his enthusiasm with the Kwango mule kick. Expertly timed, his heel connected with the wrestler's jaw. The man jerked back and sat down dazed. The crowd roared.

Patiently, Orylos waited until his opponent had recovered his wits—though by the rules of the Games he need not have done so. The man picked himself up, shook his head, cleared his wits, and charged. Again, Orylos delivered the Kwango treatment. He turned sideways, waited till the right moment, then bent. The wrestler, unable to check his momentum, hurtled over Orylos's back. As he did so, Orylos straightened. The man sailed high and landed with a thud that could be heard everywhere.

Again Orylos waited. The wrestler picked himself up, swaying. He didn't feel like charging any more. So Orylos took the initiative. First he delivered a perfect head butt. By sheer will power, the wrestler remained on his feet. While he was wondering what had hit him, Orylos expertly kicked his stomach. The wrestler grunted and doubled. Orylos brought him down with a chop to the neck. The man fell, grunting, and rolled on his back.

With a great cry, Orylos leaped high in the air, bent

his leg and brought the knee crashing down on the man's exposed throat. He twitched and convulsed briefly. Then he lay still. Again the crowd roared.

Conrad winced. "Score one, Kwango. Your young friend is a good pupil. That was not nice."

Scolopen said, "My son does not shame me."

"Nor will he," said Conrad. "He is a valiant warrior."

Orylos chose the swordsman next.

"Score two, Kwango. I hope you win a lot of booze."

"Don't fret, Boss. My young friend is in good form."

The swordsman fought in the traditional Zelosian way. He stood his ground, he cut, thrusted and parried. Orylos did not fight in the traditional way. He moved lightly from side to side, causing his opponent to twist and turn and become a little unsure of his balance. They Orylos stepped back, out of range, forcing the swordsman to follow him. The warrior grunted with rage and came on; Orylos moved to the side. He repeated these tactical maneuvres several times.

"He's teaching that character the art of mobile warfare," explained Kwango, "and getting him steamed up at the same time. Then, he'll get careless."

But it was Orylos who got careless first. He came in too close, only halfparried a lunge at his throat, and got pricked in his shoulder. A cry of dismay came from the crowd, now wholly on the side of Orylos. But the wound was not deep and not on the shoulder of the sword arm.

Orylos sprang back, forcing the swordsman to come after him. Again he moved back, and again. Now it was the turn of his opponent, who had drawn blood, to be overconfident. Once more, Orylos stepped back, and the man charged, sword raised for a slashing stroke at the neck. But, as he did so, Orylos suddenly lunged. His arm straightenèd as if it were a compressed steel spring that had suddenly been released. The blade of his sword flashed briefly in the sunlight, looking for one split second as if arm and sword had been welded together to become a two-metre lance. Because of his momentum, the swordsman could not halt his advance in time. The sword penetrated his chest and its bloody point passed through to emerge from between his shoulders. Swaying drunkenly, he fell on his back, mortally wounded. He lay motionless, the sword sticking out of him vertically, vibrating as if it had pinned him to the ground.

The crowd was beside itself. Men roared and shouted and stamped.

"Score two, Kwango," said Conrad. "But your friend had me worried for a moment or two."

"Boss, he had me worried, too," confessed Kwango. "I taught him to box clever, but he almost got too clever."

Conrad spoke to Scolopen. "I hear the voice of your people, Scolopen. Is there one among them who still does not think that Orylos is a great warrior?"

The dead swordsman was being trundled from the arena. Orylos sat down on the ground, breathing heavily. He was obviously tired. Blood, oozing from the shoulder wound, had turned his arm red.

"My son is great once more in the eyes of my people," said Scolopen. "For this alone, the Lord Kwango is already as my brother." He sighed. "There yet remains the axe . . . I know the axeman. He has never been defeated."

Indira spoke to Scolopen. "May I attend your son? I am skilled in dealing with wounds."

"It is not permitted, Lady. According to the rules of the Games, if Orylos can stand, he must still fight."

Orylos could stand, and did so. He lifted his axe. But he held the great battle-axe only with one hand. A hush descended over the amphitheatre.

The axeman made no move. He shrugged as if to say: why must I execute a wounded man? According to the rules of the Games, he could attack as soon as Orylos lifted his weapon. But he waited, perhaps confident of victory, perhaps reluctant to attack an injured man, perhaps to give Orylos time to recover his strength.

The tension grew. Orylos shook his head once or twice, as if to clear his mind. Then he gazed at the huge axeman, leaning patiently on the haft of his terrible weapon. He raised his own axe in salute, as if acknowledging the courtesy he had received. The axeman responded, both blades flashing as the weapons executed a graceful arc.

The men moved warily towards each other. Compared to his opponent, Orylos—a magnificent young man by

Terran standards—seemed small, slightly built.

It looked as if the axeman were determined to end the contest quickly—whether for the benefit of his reputation, or because he took no pleasure in challenging a wounded man, no one would ever know.

Suddenly, his axe swung low and he struck with fantastic speed at Orylos's legs. Orylos leaped high and the blade whistled beneath him. The axeman seemed surprised. He tried again. The same thing happened. Orylos himself did not try to attack. He waited.

The huge axeman gripped his weapon more firmly with both hands. He feinted for the legs once more, then used his great strength to swing the axe up, hoping to catch Orylos in midair. Orylos crouched, and the axe whistled past his ears.

Then, suddenly, he straightened up, pointed into the air with his bloody arm, and gave a great shout as if he had seen something terrible. The astounded axeman automatically followed his gaze. It gave Orylos the moment he needed. With a mighty one-handed chop, he sank the axe into his opponent's chest.

The big man staggered, and looked down in amazement at his life blood pulsing from the dreadful wound. With a supreme effort, he lifted his own axe once more and raised it high in the air for the kind of downstroke that would cut a man in two. Orylos was spent. He, too, was swaying. He didn't seem to know what was happening, didn't seem to know that the shadow of death was over his head.

The amphitheatre was hushed. For what seemed like an eternity, the two warriors faced each other, one already mortally wounded, the other dazed and weak.

The huge axeman's shoulder muscles bulged as, dying, he prepared to split the skull of the now defenceless Orylos.

He never made the stroke.

He just gave a great cry and crumpled, falling into a pool of his own blood.

There was a silence. Then suddenly, everyone in the amphitheatre was standing, shouting, waving. The King's son had defeated the Mortal Three. The very noise brought Orylos back to his senses. He turned towards Scolopen, raised his axe, and executed the royal salute.

Kwango glanced at Conrad. "Boss, you just seen the five-star Kwango touch."

"That's the oldest trick in the book. It's a once-off."

"It only had to work once," said Kwango with dignity. "I'm going to love drinking at your expense."

The noise in the amphitheatre seemed as if it would never stop. "Orylos!" "Orylos." "Orylos, Warrior of Warriors!"

Scolopen had to shout to make himself heard. "Lord Kwango, it has come to pass as you said. You are my brother. Tonight, the bards will make songs and where Orylos, son of Scolopen, chooses to walk, all men will stand aside."

"Scolopen," said Kwango, "your son was my enemy and became my friend. My friend lives and is honoured. I am content."

The Emperor smiled. "Thus speaks a man. On your world, are there many such as you?"

Kwango grinned and shook his head. "I am the first and the last of my kind."

Scolopen was puzzled. He turned to Conrad. "Can this be so?"

"There is only one Kwango," said Conrad heavily. "For which, let us all be grateful."

Phase Nine

THE MAGNIFICENT THREE

It took some time for the tumult to die down, but when it did, Amyako, son of Tostig and the last of the challengers came into the arena. Three new warriors awaited him.

He was unlucky.

He was unlucky for two reasons: first, the crowd didn't

really care, being still bemused by the feat of Orylos; and second, he made the wrong choice. He chose the axeman first.

It was over in seconds. The axeman evaded a volley of strikes and, when Amyako was weakened from his exertions, struck once only. The luckless challenger was carried from the arena minus a leg. Few of the spectators seemed to care or notice.

By now, the sun was high and the day had become very warm. Soon it would be midday—at which time a series of non-mortal events—running, jumping, wrestling —would begin. At which time also, most of the spectators would be content to take wine and food and perhaps doze somewhat, until the next sequence of mortal events began.

But before that lull, there was one more mortal event which, as Scolopen assured Conrad, ought to be quite entertaining. It was known as The Five Fatal Leaps.

While the herald announced the event, and while groups of men went into the arena and swept sand away to reveal rows of planks which they rapidly removed, Scolopen explained about The Five Fatal Leaps.

"It is the way our young men test their courage, their strength and their judgement, Conrad. As you now see, there are five pits in the arena, each five paces wide, each ten paces from the next pit. The first is the pit of serpents, the second is the pit of wild animals, the third is the pit of sharpened stakes, the fourth is the pit of water, the fifth is the pit of fire."

As he spoke, a torch was put to the liquid in the fifth pit. It began to burn instantly. Conrad's first thought was: so they have petroleum on Zelos. I must get that confirmed and radio back to Terra. Then he gazed intently at the line of rectangular pits in the centre of the arena.

"How deep are the pits, Scolopen?"

"Twice a man's height. If any man should fall into any pit, he will fall into the arms of Vallin."

"What about the water pit?" asked Kwango. "It might be a good thing to get wet before you jump over the pit of fire."

Scolopen gave a thin smile. "Kwango, my brother, in

154

the water pit there are hundreds of small fish that can rip the flesh from the bone before a man has time to cry out."

"Piranha!" exclaimed Kwango.

Conrad tapped Lieutenant Smith on the shoulder. "Can you do it?"

"Try me."

"Good. Then it's time we showed the flag."

The herald had just announced that there were seven contestants.

Conrad turned to Scolopen. "There are now eight contestants. The Lady Indira wearies of inaction. She will take The Five Fatal Leaps."

Scolopen was appalled. "No woman has ever attempted this thing. It is impossible! Each year many men die. No woman has ever been permitted to enter any event in the Games."

Conrad smiled. "Scolopen, as you know, in our world, the Lady Indira ranks as an Immortal. Let her compete. There is a time for change in the history of all peoples. It has now come to your race. Let her compete. She will not dishonour our people."

Scolopen seemed bewildered. "So be it," he said. "Your very coming has already changed our ways. Also, I am indebted to the Lord Kwango."

He rose and spoke to the herald. "Let it be known to all present that the Lady Indira, ranking as an Immortal in her own land, desires to take The Five Fatal Leaps. I have spoken."

Mingled cries of surprise and derision came from the amphitheatre. Then there was some hesitant laughter.

Haruken, fully armed, appeared in the arena. He faced Scolopen. "Scolopen, King and Emperor," he said, "do you so love the Outlanders that you will allow them to corrupt our ancient ways?"

There was a great silence. No man had dared to speak so insolently to Scolopen before.

"You, also, corrupt our ancient ways, Haruken. Were this not the day of the Games, I would have your head. Fear not, there will be an accounting. Before the sun sets, Haruken, doubtless you will speak to me again."

Haruken saluted. "If Vallin wills it, Scolopen, I will speak to you again."

Conrad suddenly saw a solution to his problem. He, too, stood up. "Scolopen, King and Emperor," he said in a loud voice, "I weary of this dog. Before all present, I acknowledge that you are Emperor of the Known World and I hope that there will be peace always between your great people and mine."

He paused for effect, and gazed down at Haruken. "But truly I weary of this dog's ill-omened barking. Moreover, he has the aspect of an ill-bred hound—vicious and cunning, but without loyalty to his master. Therefore, I ask myself an interesting question. Does he also have the heart of a dog, or has Vallin—in pity—graced him with the heart of a man?"

The silence that followed was electric, like the charged atmosphere before a storm.

Scolopen was amazed. Haruken's face darkened with anger and his body shook with uncontrollable rage. For a while, he could not trust himself to speak.

Eventually, he managed to gain some control. "Outlander, it is plain that you weary of living. Your death is in your words. So be it. Know that of all the Immortals, I rank the highest, having killed seventeen men in fair combat."

"I grieve for those bitten by a mad dog," said Conrad pleasantly. "Doubtless the infection was rapid."

Haruken literally danced with rage in the arena.

Kwango said softly, "Boss, I think you are getting through to him."

"Outlander!" shouted Haruken, "I challenge you to mortal combat. I have seen you strike with the hand. Let all present see how you fare with morningstar and sword."

"Scolopen," said Conrad, ignoring the outburst, "I am a guest in your land, and so far as I can, I respect your customs and your laws. Is it permitted that I teach this dog new tricks?"

The King appeared quite puzzled by Conrad's behaviour. "Words have been said that, in these lands, can only lead to the duel. It is my wish that this duel shall be an event of the Games. Haruken is already committed to

156

the three mortal events wherein, if he triumphs, he could become Winner of the Games. After these events, the duel may take place."

Conrad saw instantly what the wily King was up to. There were three chances that Haruken could be killed or injured. But if he survived, much of his strength would be used up.

"Scolopen, there can be little honour for me in facing Haruken when he is weary. Moreover, if he is killed in the mortal events, he will have gone to the arms of Vallin before giving me satisfaction. And if he is wounded, I cannot fight him."

Before the King could answer, Haruken shouted, "The Outlander is in a hurry to die. Grant his wish, Scolopen, lest it be seen that for love of the Outlanders, you are not fit to be Emperor."

Scolopen gazed down at him in wrath. "On any day but this, Haruken, as I have said, such words would separate your head from your body. I grant the wish of the Lord Conrad of the Silver Patch. I have spoken." With a wave of his hand, Scolopen dismissed Haruken.

"But first," said Conrad, "let us see how the Lady Indira fares in the Fatal Five. The result may be of interest to the dog down there that snarls."

"It shall be." Scolopen still looked very puzzled.

Conrad patted Indira on the back. "Get down there, love, and do your thing."

"How do you want it played?"

"Go last. Don't demoralize the others by making it seem too easy. O.K.?"

"O.K., James. I hope you know what you are doing in taking on Haruken."

Conrad grinned. "So do I. I haven't the faintest notion how to use morningstar and sword. But Haruken doesn't know what my tin arm can do. So, perhaps, we equalize."

The Five Fatal Leaps was a spectacular event. The first contestant cleared the pit of serpents easily but mistimed his run to leap the pit of wild animals. He fell in a heap against the edge, one foot dangling. A creature resembling a puma leaped high against the wall of the pit and dragged him down. Mercifully, his screams were short-lived. The second contestant cleared the pit of serpents, the pit of wild animals, and the pit of sharpened stakes, all of which apparently tired him. He took the water pit too slowly. There were no screams and only a few bubbles before the water turned red.

Only two of the seven Zelossians entered for the event cleared the course. One of them was a superb athlete with excellent nerve and timing. The other was just plain lucky. He almost fell into the pit of stakes and the pit of water. The near disasters seemed to give him strength. He cleared the fire pit easily. Of the casualties, three perished in the water pit, one in the animal pit, and one in the fire.

The amphitheatre became quiet as Indira prepared to jump. It was all over very quickly. She took only a short run, but seemed to build up tremendous speed. She jumped, not as if she were jumping pits five metres wide, but as if she were in a hurdles event. Her speed and grace were astounding, as was her precision. She jumped high over the fire—far higher than any other competitor—they had had to leap through the flames. She cleared them easily.

The silence continued for a moment or two. Then the applause was deafening. Indira bowed gracefully towards Scolopen—then leaped all five pits again. Conrad frowned. That, he thought, was overdoing it.

"The Lady Indira is as a bird," said Scolopen thoughtfully. "That feat has been attempted but once before. He who attempted it perished on the seventh leap."

"The Lady Indira is a remarkable woman," said Conrad gravely. "I go, now, to meet Haruken. If I should fall, Scolopen, you will escort my companions safely to the starship?"

"By the life of Orylos, to whom the Lord Kwango gave the gift of greatness, it shall be done." He smiled. "But I think you will not fall. The legs of the Lady Indira and the right arm of Conrad of the Silver Patch have the same magic, I think."

"What magic is that?"

"The magic of steel and fire."

"Kimatun?" said Conrad.

The King nodded. "The ear of Scolopen listens well."

Conrad passed Indira on his way down to the arena. "You overdid it," he accused.

"I'm sorry, James. I couldn't resist the opportunity of shaking these people's notions about the role of women. . . . Take care."

Conrad shrugged. "Morningstar and sword. Not my scene, really. But don't worry. I'll get rid of some of the hardware pretty fast."

Haruken, fully armoured and with his weapons, was waiting for him.

The herald proclaimed the event. "Mortal combat, sword and morningstar, between Lord Conrad of the Silver Patch and Haruken, captain of Immortals, who has dispatched seventeen men to the arms of Vallin."

Haruken said, "Where is your armour, Outlander?"

"I need no armour."

"Where, then, are your weapons?"

"I have no weapons. Will you permit me to borrow some?"

Haruken laughed. "You are brave, Outlander. That is something. A man should be familiar with his own weapons." He raised his voice. "Sword and morningstar for the dog-tamer!"

Orylos brought them. "These are mine, Lord Conrad." He gazed coldly at Haruken. "Use them well . . . It was Haruken who caused your sister to be returned to you in the manner you saw."

"Thank you for the weapons and for this news, Orylos. Both are welcome."

"Orylos, this I will remember," snarled Haruken. "I will remember it when the Outlander lies at my feet." He turned to Conrad. "Well, Outlander, take up your weapons. I weary of delay." He glanced angrily at Orylos, who was leaving the arena to the two men.

Conrad picked up the two weapons, the sword in his biohand, the morningstar in his prosthetic hand. The sword, fortunately, was light and could be wielded comfortably with one hand. The only trouble was that Conrad knew nothing of swordmanship.

The morningstar was a crude but deadly instrument. Its thick, leather-bound haft had perhaps half a metre of sturdy chain attached to the top. On the other end of the chain was a spiked steel ball, as large as a grapefruit.

The thing to do, he decided, was to lose the sword as soon as possible, so that he could concentrate on one weapon. Also, the encounter would have to be brief, since time was on the side of Haruken's skill and experience.

"Are you ready, Outlander? It is a rule of the Games and of the duel, that no man must strike until his opponent signifies that he is prepared for combat."

"I am ready, Haruken. Vallin is impatient for your company."

The two men circled warily. I must keep my distance for a while, thought Conrad. He knows I am not used to these things. Let him get the idea I'm turning chicken.

Haruken whirled his morningstar threateningly, then lunged with the sword. Conrad retreated nimbly. Again, Haruken advanced. The huge Zelosian was full of confidence. Again he lunged. This time Conrad attempted to parry with the sword. Haruken's sword arm was stronger and more dextrous than his. Haruken twisted expertly, Conrad's blade was forced aside, and the point of Haruken's sword penetrated the bioarm between elbow and shoulder.

It was not deep, and strangely, Conrad felt no pain. Adrenalin, he thought vaguely. It cancels the pain message in the stress of battle. He did not let go of his sword.

"First blood!" roared Haruken.

There were cries of dismay and encouragement from the spectators. Some shouted, "Haruken!" But some also shouted, "Conrad."

"Last blood counts," said Conrad. "Your mother was an evil-smelling bitch and you were sired on a dung heap."

With a great shout of rage, Haruken swept his sword down on Conrad's blade and dashed it from the now-weakened fingers.

"Pick it up, Outlander," he hissed. "I will not strike. The people already know that you are no match for me."

Conrad was quite relieved that he had lost the sword so convincingly. Now he could concentrate.

"I do not need a sword," he said. "A man does not

need a sword to put down a dog."

Haruken flung his own sword down. "Nor do I need one to put down an Outlander."

Conrad smiled. "That is a mistake you will regret." He lifted his morningstar and caused the spiked ball to whirl so rapidly that it whistled as it passed through the air.

Haruken stepped back and gazed at him openmouthed. No man that the Zelosian had ever known had the strength of arm to do that.

While Haruken was still wondering, Conrad passed the haft of his morningstar to his biohand, and let the heavy weapon hang by his side, the spiked ball resting on the ground.

"Why do you do that?" Haruken was totally confused.

"Because the time has come for you to die," retorted Conrad tranquilly. "Before that happens, Haruken, know this. My sister requires vengeance, and it is necessary for you to die in a spectacular fashion. Then there will be peace between our two races."

Haruken did not seem to know what to do. An almost defenceless man stood before him, a wounded man who had transferred his remaining weapon to the weakened arm, while at the same time, confidently threatening him with destruction. And Haruken did not know what to do.

"Your mother was a hellbitch," taunted Conrad. "She was in heat for every dog that scented her."

With a great cry of rage, Haruken lifted his morningstar and whirled the spiked ball, aiming for Conrad's head.

It never connected.

Conrad's prosthetic hand shot up in a blur of action and caught the ball perfectly. He snatched it in midflight and held it steady. It was as if it had embedded itself in a wall. There was no sign of blood or injury on the hand. Haruken was dumbfounded. Conrad jerked the ball toward him, snapping the chain, and leaving the haft of the weapon in Haruken's hand.

The Zelosian gazed at him, hypnotized.

"My sister sends her greeting, Haruken," said Conrad. "Vallin awaits your coming."

Then he hurled the spiked morningstar with such force and accuracy that Haruken's head was separated from his body, and the mangled wreck carried to the far side of the arena.

Though there were one or two mortal and a number of non-mortal events to follow, the rest of the Games seemed rather like an anticlimax to the spectators. This was a day to remember. They had seen the King's son defeat the Mortal Three, the Lady Indira leap the Five Fatal Pits *twice* and live, and they had seen the mightiest warrior of the Immortals killed instantly in a way that would live in song and legend.

As he stood by the headless body, Conrad judged it was a time for diplomacy. "Scolopen, King and Emperor," he said in a loud voice, so that all could hear, "let none say that Haruken lacked courage or gallantry, only that he lacked wisdom. Remember the great warrior. Forget the fool."

The King made answer. "Lord Conrad of the Silver Patch, you are generous to the fellow. As you request, so it shall be."

Conrad bowed and returned to his place by Scolopen's side.

"What about that wound?" asked Indira.

"Cancel query," snapped Conrad. "You can get professional later. Just now, I'm supposed to be Superman."

Orylos had entered for two more mortal events and several non-mortal events. But his opponents in the mortal events withdrew, thus conceding victory, not wishing to face one who had triumphed over the Mortal Three. Their position was untenable, as they and the crowd well knew. If either of them killed Orylos, he would have to answer to the mob. And if they did not, they were dead men anyway.

When the non-mortal running and leaping events were announced, Scolopen said drily to Indira, "Lady, do not enter, I beg of you. I have no desire to see our young men shamed."

"Your wish is my command," she answered. "Also, I see that Orylos has entered for these events. Be proud

162

of your son, Scolopen. He is destined for greatness."

Orylos took the long jump, the high jump, and the Zelosian equivalent of the hundred metres. He lost the distance runs, doubtless because his strength was spent.

The Games ended as they had begun—with a bloodbath. Ten men from one town disputed grazing rights with ten men from another. The sole survivor of the conflict saluted Scolopen and gained the verdict before he fell and died from loss of blood.

The sun sank over the amphitheatre. As it did so, the judges conferred together. Then the herald came to announce their verdict.

"Be it known to all present, Orylos, son of Scolopen, having dismissed the Mortal Three, having gained two conceded victories in other mortal events, and having won three non-mortal events, is now and before all people proclaimed Winner of the Games."

The uproar was deafening. Orylos walked to the centre of the arena and turned to face Scolopen.

"Scolopen, King and Emperor, I salute you."

Scolopen rose and went through the ancient ritual. "Orylos, Winner of the Games, do you seek to challenge my power and authority? If so, name your weapons."

Orylos knelt. "Scolopen, King and Emperor, I make no challenge. I know that you rule wisely and I will obey you in all matters until—the Games." It was the ancient answer of acceptance.

The crowd went wild.

Then the sun sank low, its last rays hitting the polished mirror at the far end of the arena. The light was reflected to the figure of a single trumpeter.

When the last trumpet sounds had died, the torches were lit.

Conrad turned to Scolopen. "Went the day well?"

"Thou knowest, Lord Conrad, that the day went well. Yesternight, I was in a black mood, foreseeing the death of my son and also my own death. Now, my enemy is dead and my son is Winner of the Games. Much of this, as I know, is due to you and your companions. What gift can I bestow on you?"

"Only the gift of friendship, Scolopen. Whatever the

future holds, let there be peace between your race and mine."

Scolopen laughed. "You are a persistent man, Conrad."

"So I have been told."

Phase Ten

THE KWANGO SCENARIOS

The five Expendables were escorted back to the *Santa Maria* by a squadron of Immortals, led by Scolopen himself. After the Games, they had spent three more days in Rossvallin. Ideally, Conrad would have preferred to wander about freely, seeing how the ordinary people lived, visiting the markets, watching the craftsmen at work. But that proved impossible. Wherever he went, the people thronged to see him and touch him. They had begun to call him Lord of the Morningstar—which, he reflected, was not entirely inappropriate. Women asked him to lay his right hand on the right hand of their male children—doubtless hoping that the magic might prove contagious. Men gave him the royal salute. Warriors hurriedly laid down their weapons at his approach—thus indicating in Zelosian terms their refusal to offer offence, take offence, or accept a challenge.

It got so bad that Conrad could not go anywhere without an escort of Immortals to keep back those who wished to touch him, speak with him, and offer him gifts. Kwango and Lieutenant Smith fared little better. Kwango was persuaded to visit the School of Wrestling, a kind of gymnasium where the "beardless ones" disciplined themselves and trained their bodies for the rigours of manhood. By the time he left, the Zelosian art of wrestling had been transformed.

Lieutenant Smith was idolized by the women. For Zelosian centuries, they had been regarded as "things." Things for pleasure, things for procreation, things for work. But, because of Indira's performance at the Games, the women were beginning to question their ancient and degrading role. One woman had symbolically shown the way. The long fight for women's emancipation had been triggered.

Gautier and Ustinov were lucky. They were able to explore Rossvallin without too much difficulty. But even Immortals stood aside for them, being unsure as to what special powers they might also possess, and being unwilling to find out.

Now, as Conrad descended from the chariot that had brought the Expendables back to the *Santa Maria*, he felt reasonably satisfied that participation in the War Games had produced the desired result.

He spoke to Scolopen. "I thank you for your kindness and your hospitality. I believe we now understand each other well. Scolopen, King and Emperor of the Known World, Triple Winner of the Games, I salute you, knowing that you are a wise man."

"Conrad of the Silver Patch," Scolopen smiled, "Lord of the Morningstar, I salute you also. The days together went well."

"Would you care to see inside the vessel that brought us from beyond the sky? We can serve food to refresh you and your Immortals."

Scolopen shook his head. "Conrad, we are a simple but a proud people. We are not yet ready to learn of the miracles that may one day humble us. Give us time. As for food and drink, we have our own and are content. It is enough."

Scolopen tapped the transceiver that Conrad had given him and taught him to use. "We will talk again presently, will we not?"

"We will talk soon, Scolopen. May you have a good journey back to Rossvallin."

"You will tell me when you hear from the wise men of your world? You will tell me if more of your people wish to come here, in vessels such as this?"

"I will tell you. I will tell you the truth."

"That I do not doubt. The Lord Conrad is known throughout the land to be a man of his word. Farewell."

Scolopen signalled. The column of Immortals wheeled, and wheeled again. Scolopen swung his pulpul round and rode to the head of the column. Then they galloped north at great speed.

"Boss," said Kwango, "I am now going to catch up on all that booze you owe me."

"Kurt, you are going to catch up on some work first. In less than sixty days from now, we should get an answer from Terra. Before then there is a lot to be done. For starters, I want an indepth ecological survey of one million square kilometres. Then I want seismic surveys, projections of potential mineral, metals and fossil fuels supplies. You can have Hal and Jean-Pierre and maybe a couple of robots to help you. Then, if you have any time on your hands—"

"Boss," said Kwango bleakly, "not only are you a real mean bastard, but you just ain't got no heart."

Conrad grinned. "I'm glad you finally got to the truth . . . You can do *some* boozing tonight—but not until you have treated us to the Kwango scenario."

"I talk better when I'm drinking."

"O.K., black man, we'll see."

That evening, all the Expendables took dinner together in the saloon, while Matthew stood watch on the nav deck at the command screens, and a couple of robots patrolled the compound. It was unlikely that there would be any more trouble from the Zelosians, and it was virtually impossible for any wild animal to get into the stockade. Conrad realized he was being somewhat overcautious, but better safe than sorry.

The meal was excellent. Zelosian food. Fish with brown flesh that tasted like salmon, grilled pulpul steaks, and vegetables that tasted like tomatoes but did not look at all like them. To follow, there was an assortment of delicious wild fruits. Evidently, Hildegarde Dolfuss had been very busy analyzing the specimens she had collected, and then checking upon their acceptability by the human digestive and metabolic processes.

She looked, now, to be fully recovered from her ordeal. Conrad watched her across the dinner table, animatedly chatting with Kwango. She seemed happy and relaxed.

Yes, thought Conrad, the meal was excellent. Good Zelosian food. But the wine in his glass—the rich red wine —was Châteauneuf-du-Pape, one of the great wines of Earth.

He lifted his glass and stared at it, thinking of the grapes that had been pressed so many light-years away. Indira also lifted her glass. She seemed to divine what he was thinking.

"Applecross," she said softly, and put the glass to her lips.

"Applecross," said Conrad, smiling, and drank also.

Kwango glanced at them both and rolled his eyes. Conrad caught his expression and instantly cancelled the images that were forming in his mind.

"Before we all get maudlin," said Conrad, acknowledging his sin, "the illustrious Kwango will solve the problem that has been baffling us all—how it happens that there are already human beings here on Zelos."

"Boss," said Kwango, pouring himself another drink, "I got two solutions. And you ain't going to like either of them. So fasten your seat belt."

"Kurt," said Hildegard, "it is far too early for any responsible scientist to attempt to formulate theories of origin."

"Hildegarde, you lovely woman, I am not a responsible scientist," he retorted. "I am the one and only Kwango. . . . Are you sitting comfortably, children? Then I'll begin.

"Both theories have one common implication—which is necessary if we are to make any sense out of the problem at all. Somewhere in dis little ole galaxy, folks, there has to be a race as far ahead of us in science and technology as we are ahead of that stupid guy who invented the wheel. Also, folks, there has to be other planets where crazy human beings chop each other to pieces or try to poison themselves by environmental pollution. Small cosmos, ain't it?"

"Kurt, don't overdo the funnies," said Conrad. "We have all had a strenuous time."

"Boss, don't cramp my style. O.K., I know you are all tired, so I'll give it to you fast. These Zelosians are definitely human, and the chances of them evolving exactly like us—well, there ain't no chances. The idea is absurd. So, Scenario One states that maybe fifty to one hundred thousand years ago, some galactic eggheads touched down on Sol Three and took samples of the most intelligent animals they found there. They thought it would be fun to try a few experiments that wouldn't cost them too much. So they dumped some of the specimens here on Zelos, and maybe on other E-type planets, just for the hell of it. Then they hot rodded back through the light-years to play games somewhere else. . . . That, ladies and gents, is the Kwango Scenario One."

"What the hell are you drinking, Kurt?" asked Hal derisively.

Jane Ustinov laughed. "That's sheer fantasy."

"Why fifty to one hundred thousand years ago?" asked Hildegard. She was not laughing.

"I was hoping you would ask. That was when *homo* was just getting demonstrably *sapien*. The visitors observed the critter—probably ran extrapolations of its potential through whatever they used for computers—and decided to give it a chance in other favourable environments. Maybe in case it eventually managed to destroy its natural home—which it almost has."

"Scenario One has the authentic Kwango style," observed Conrad drily. "It's way out. But maybe it is easier to believe than parallel evolution. The flora and fauna of Zelos are different from those of Earth. So why the hell should the people be the same?"

"Not quite the same," pointed out Jean-Pierre. "What of their size?"

"They are huge, certainly," said Indira, "but not outside the normal human parameter. We have tall races on Earth, and we also have pygmies."

"Before we discuss the finer points," said Conrad, "let's have Scenario Two."

"Boss, you are going to love it even less. According to Scenario Two, those galactic clever boys touched down on Terra, Zelos, and maybe a few more planets approximately two million years ago. And how do you like that?"

"I don't. And I warned you not to make with the funnies."

"I am not making with the funnies." Kwango sounded pained.

Hildegarde leaned forward. "Why two million years, Kurt?"

Kwango seemed to ignore her question. "Let me tell you about my dear old granddaddy—on my mother's side. He was a gardener. Yes, folks, a very good gardener. He ran an estate and made things grow where they had no right to grow at all. You see, he was a real cunning old man. He *tailored* his plants to their environment. Bred and crossbred until he got the right strain. Then he'd nurture the young plants in his hothouse, then he'd harden them off, then he'd plant them where people least expected to see them grow and flourish. He was also a great joker, was my dead old granddaddy. The first man to grow oranges and lemons on the same tree. The first man to develop the pineapple-flavoured banana, the noncrying onion, and the nutty nectarine. He had a lot of firsts and he also had style. I've been told I take after him."

Conrad raised his prosthetic arm threateningly. "You are running out of time, black man."

"White trash, sir, you are missing de point."

Again Hildegarde said, "Why two million years?"

Kwango beamed at her, "My darling Hildegarde, you are the only one who's been listening to dis pore nigra. You know, of course, that despite our late friend Charles and his peculiar notions, nobody ever did establish the existence of the so-called missing link?"

"I am familiar with Darwinian theory. . . . So that is why two million years."

"Give the lady a cigar! Friends, I am now able to disclose that no one has yet conclusively *proved* man's descent from the primates. Interesting. It leaves room for maneuvre, as de diplomats would say."

"Kwango!" Conrad was really getting angry now.

"O.K., Boss. Cool it. I've had my fun. Scenario Two. Picture the galactic gardeners at their honest toil. They breed special bedding plants—or, more accurately, critters —in a computer controlled hothouse, about a thousand light years past morning. Then they skim through the galaxy, looking for suitable gardens. And they fix it all to look real natural. End of story."

There was a silence. Conrad poured himself another drink very carefully. Châteauneuf-du-Pape, the rich red wine of Earth. What Kwango said was nonsense, of course. And yet . . . And yet . . .

Other people poured drinks. Nobody spoke. The silence lengthened.

Eventually, Conrad could stand it no longer. The implications of Scenario Two were horrendous and humiliating.

"Kwango, you black bastard, you've flipped. You're over the hill. Lieutenant Smith will prepare a medical and psychiatric report. I will recommend an honourable discharge."

Kwango shrugged. "Yes, suh, Massa Boss. Permission to continue drinking?"

"Permission granted."

"It's possible," said Indira reluctantly. "It's just possible."

"My God!" exclaimed Hildegarde. "Kurt is mad, brilliant—or both. How else can we explain it?"

Kwango swallowed his drink and poured another. He drank that very rapidly, too.

Conrad gazed at him. "Kurt, I know you. You are holding something back. What is it?"

"Boss, you don't want to share my nightmares."

"Try me."

"Then don't complain if you don't sleep too well hereafter. . . . Assume a high probability rating for Scenario Two."

"So?"

"So if you were a gardener and you'd taken the trouble to put plants in a strange soil far from your hothouse, what would be your next step?"

"I'd come back later to see how they were doing." Suddenly, Conrad was appalled. He was appalled by the mental vision of a master race, jetting down in starships through the skies of Earth and Zelos and, possibly, planets elsewhere.

170

"Score one, Commander, sir." Kwango poured himself yet another drink. "Now comes the sixty-four thousand solar question: are we the gardener's plants or are we his or their children? Permission to pass out?"

"Permission granted," said Conrad. Suddenly, he felt very cold.

Kwango finished his drink, gazed at Conrad with eyes out of focus, then slumped.

Again, there was a long silence.

END GAME

A reply came from Terra just seventy-nine days after Conrad had sent Kwango's report. It came late in the afternoon when Conrad, armed with a laser rifle, was taking a stroll outside the perimeter.

Lieutenant Smith was out in the hovercar with Ustinov and the robot Paul, exploring the terrain a hundred kilometres to the south. She had orders to be back before sunset. Dolfuss was inside the stockade, taking it easy in a hammock, catching the sun. A small speck in the western sky, and the faint sound of the chopper's engines told Conrad that Kwango and Mencken were returning from Square Thirty-nine in the million square kilometre survey block. At this rate, Conrad estimated that it would take them at least another sixty Z-days to work through the hundred squares into which the survey area had been divided. Already, they had verified the existence of substantial deposits of petroleum, iron and nickel. Zelos, it seemed, was rich in natural resources.

Matthew's voice came over the transceiver. "Matthew to Commander Conrad. Do you read me?"

"I read you. Over."

"I have recorded a transmission from Terra. Shall I channel it direct to you?"

"No. Bring me a printout. I want a little time to think."

"Decision noted. Execution proceeds."

Conrad gazed around him. Zelos was a very attractive world, really. The best yet. He wouldn't mind settling here himself. A man could do worse than take up the simple life—hunting, shooting, fishing . . . A small farm, maybe . . . Children . . . That made him think of Indira, and that time at Applecross. He cancelled the thought hastily. Expendables don't have children, because Expendables are . . . expendable.

' There was a hiduminium cross on a small hill about a hundred metres away. Conrad walked towards it. He often went there when he had time to kill and no one else was present. He always found fresh flowers there. He knew who brought them. Jane Ustinov. But he never saw her do it. Probably, she got up early to gather the flowers while they were fresh with dew, and before the day's duties claimed her. Beneath the cross lay the body of Jean-Pierre Gautier. He had died just twenty-seven days ago, saving Jane from the attack of a suddenly enraged wild pulpul.

Jane, wearing only her bra, had stumbled back to the stockade in a state of hysteria and near collapse. Gautier's body—what was left of it—was also unclothed. It had been a beautiful afternoon. Both of them had been off duty. Conrad never enquired why they broke the rules and told no one where they were going. The reason was obvious.

He came to the cross and read the legend cut into the hiduminium: "Jean-Pierre Gautier, native of Earth, nationality French, Expendable, gave his life for a comrade in the proving of Zelos."

It was a fair statement. Conrad had chosen the words himself.

"Well, Jean-Pierre, Terra has uttered. What's the message, *mon brave*? Will they let us prove for colonization, or will they tell us to get the hell out and not step on the daisies? Anyway, I hope you had much pleasure with Jane before that damned animal got rough . . . I don't like the score. You are dead simply because some stupid animal got excited, and Hildegarde is pregnant because some bloody Zelosians had a gang bang. Maybe it's all my fault. Maybe I'm getting old."

Matthew interrupted his soliloquy. "Here is the print-out, Commander, as you requested."

Conrad took the piece of paper. "You picked a bad time to deliver it, Matthew."

"I am sorry, Commander. Query: What would have been a good time?"

"Cancel statement, Matthew. Return to the *Santa Maria*. Call Lieutenant Smith and have her confirm that she will return before sunset."

"Decisions noted. Execution proceeds."

Conrad read the message.

FROM DIRECTOR EX-PEND TO CONRAD. YOURS AC-KNOWLEDGED. PROVING OPERATIONS TO CEASE FORTH-WITH. ZELOS WILL NOT BE COLONIZED IN FORESEEABLE FUTURE BECAUSE OF EXISTENCE OF INDIGENOUS INTEL-LIGENT HUMANOID LIFE-FORMS AS DEFINED IN YOURS. NOW PROCEED AS FOLLOWS. ONE, CONSTRUCT ACCOM-MODATION FOR APPROX TWO HUNDRED SCIENTISTS, SPECIALISTS, OBSERVERS, DIPLOMATS. THEY WILL MAKE STUDY OF ZELOSIAN CULTURE AND WILL ADVISE ON FUTURE POSSIBILITIES OF COLONIZATION. IMPERATIVE SCIENTIFIC FACILITIES AVAILABLE. TWO, CANNIBALIZE EQUIPMENT OF *Santa Maria* FOR AFOREMENTIONED AS JUDGED NECESSARY. THREE, SIGNAL WHEN READY TO RECEIVE AFOREMENTIONED TWO HUNDRED INVESTIGA-TORS BY MATTER TRANSMISSION. FOUR, UPON COM-PLETION, RETURN TERRA EARLIEST. ACKNOWLEDGE. MESSAGE ENDS."

"Damnation!" said Conrad. Then he looked at the cross. "I'm sorry, Jean-Pierre, not you . . . You did a fantastic job on the radio mines. . . . Well, I suppose I expected it. Kwango will be glad, anyway. So will Scolopen. But Jane won't be here much longer to pick those flowers."

He put the paper into his pocket, turned and walked back to the ship.

That evening, at dinner, he read the message out. Hal was the first to react.

"Kind of an anticlimax, Commander," he said.

173

"You could say that, Hal. But we all knew it was a possibility."

Kwango scratched his head. "Sorry, Boss. I know how you feel . . . But what the hell do they mean by cannibalize? I am not going to see *my* library and instruments and computer systems left behind for a bunch of no-good, white-collar workers. No bright young Ph.D. is going to collect his Nobel Prize from working on my data."

"Kurt, we are going to leave all unessential scientific equipment, records and supplies for the study team."

Hildegarde said suddenly, "I'm not going back, James."

"You're what?" Conrad couldn't believe his ears.

"I'm not going back. I'm going to stay on Zelos and join the study team."

"Dolfuss, you are an Expendable. You will obey my orders."

Hildegarde patted her belly complacently. "I'm part of the unessential equipment you are going to leave behind. I carry a child that is half-Zelosian. Your study team are going to want to see how that little experiment turns out. Also, I know you are not empowered to transport exobiological material back to the solar system without prior permission. I have a bellyful of exobiological material." She smiled. "Want to make an issue of it?"

Conrad's mouth fell open. He started to say something, but the words turned to jelly.

Kwango winced. "Oh, my Gawd! Congratulations, Hildegarde. One, you have rendered de good Commander speechless. Two, you make worse funnies than I do."

"Furthermore," said Hildegarde, "I don't think the Emperor of the Known World would approve of a child conceived on *his* land and sired by one of *his* Immortals and therefore probably one of *his* subjects being taken to the other side of the sky."

"I'm going to my cabin to talk to Scolopen." It was all Conrad could think of to say.

When he was alone, he used the transceiver. "Conrad to Scolopen. Conrad to Scolopen. Do you hear me?"

There was no response. He tried again. Still no response. Eventually Scolopen came through on the fifth attempt at contact.

"Conrad, my friend, I greet you through the magic casket, though it is not as good as if we were face to face and could see what was written thereon."

"It is not," agreed Conrad. "I have had a reply from the wise men of my world, Scolopen. They have decided not to send people to make their homes here."

"It is a good decision, Conrad. Truly, they have wisdom."

"But they wish to send people to study your ways, to learn about your people."

"How many warriors come?" Scolopen sounded suspicious.

"No warriors. Only learned men and women. No warriors, Scolopen. Those who come would be defeated by any contestant in the War Games."

Scolopen laughed. "I believe you, Conrad, knowing you to be a man of your word. They shall be made welcome. But they must not attempt to change us. That is understood?"

"That is understood." agreed Conrad. "Any who displease you will be sent back."

"I have the word of Conrad. It is enough."

"There is one more thing. My sister, she who was taken by your warriors, is with child. She wishes to remain here."

"She, too, is wise. The child will be a child of two worlds, a bond between both. Whether a girl child or a boy child, it will be raised to greatness in the eyes of my people. It will be a symbol of the peace between us. Is that enough?"

"It is enough. Presently, when the learned men and women arrive, I must leave, having done my duty."

"Shall we meet before your departure?"

"We shall, Scolopen. I will come to Rossvallin to pay my respects to the Emperor of the Known World, Triple Winner of the Games."

Scolopen laughed. "Conrad of the Silver Patch, Lord of the Morningstar, you do me too much honour. Are *you* not also Lord of the Skies?"

"I prefer to be Scolopen's friend."

"That was understood. Until we meet."

"Until we meet."

Later, Conrad walked in the compound. It was a clear night. The stars were brilliant. He thought he was alone. He wasn't.

Lieutenant Smith came up behind him and took his hand, the biohand.

"Tomorrow," said Conrad, "it's a crash programme. Exos for all except Dolfuss. There is a lot of timber to be cut, a lot of buildings to be constructed. We'll have to use four of the robots as well."

"James," she said softly.

"Kwango can plan the layout of the research centre, or whatever they want to call it. Mencken can see to water supply and general services. Ustinov can deal with the domestic side, dormitories, canteens and so on."

"James," said Indira, squeezing his hand.

"When those clever bastards come rolling out of the matter transmitter in their titanium cylinders, I want everything to be ready."

"James," said Indira, "you are one hell of a man."

"Not only is Kwango going to lose his entire data storage system," Conrad went on, "but we will also have to leave the electron microscope, the chromatography gear, the spectroanalyser, the X ray systems, the—what did you say?"

"James, you are one hell of a man. That is exactly what I said. Further data is as follows. It is a starlit night here on Zelos. I desire you to kiss me and hold me very close. We are a long way from Earth and we have to keep warm somehow."

"Decision noted," said Conrad softly. "Execution proceeds."

He took her in his arms. He felt a woman press close to him. And, suddenly, it was as if all the stars in the sky of Zelos had begun to dance . . .